# SAVE A HORSE, RIDE A VISCOUNT

## THE FOOTMEN'S CLUB SERIES

### VALERIE BOWMAN

JUNE THIRD ENTERPRISES, LLC

Print edition ISBN: 978-1-7368417-1-6

Digital edition ISBN: 978-1-7368417-0-9

Book Cover Design © Lyndsey Llewellen at Llewellen Designs.

*For my friend and writing sister (SC), Anna Bennett, for her generous help with my blurbs and her appreciation of a racy title (wink).*
*And to the cheeky reader who gave me the idea for this title.*
*YOLO!*

**His best laid plans…**

Ewan Fairchild, Viscount Clayton, has been busy ticking off the boxes for a bright future. Become a rising star in Parliament? Check. Find a lady he intends to marry? Check. Make his stables the envy of every man in London? Check, thanks to the prize Arabian thoroughbred he's just won at auction. Clayton's on his way to having it all and won't change course for anyone—not even the beautiful young woman next door.

**…are about to go awry**

Lady Theodora Ballard didn't mind missing a Season of dinner parties, balls, and soirees to care for her ailing mother, but when Thea's father sold her horse out from under her, she thought her heart would break. Now the roguishly handsome viscount at the neighboring estate has *her* horse—and she'll stop at nothing to get him back. Unfortunately, a horse spying mission goes south, leaving Thea with a broken leg and Clayton with an alluring houseguest who upends his orderly world. The sparks between them are undeniable, but secrets and scandal abound. It's going to take more than a little love to save them…

# CHAPTER ONE

*The Earl of Blackstone's Country Estate, Devon, October 1813*

"I'm going to steal that horse," Lady Theodora Ballard said as her maid, Maggie, fastened her stays.

"Are you certain that's the best way to handle the situation?" Maggie replied, sighing heavily.

Theodora shook her head. Poor, dear, sweet Maggie. She wasn't just Thea's maid. Maggie had been her closest friend since their births, which were only months apart. Maggie was the daughter of one of her mother's favorite maids. The girls had grown up together on the estate. Thea's mother—God rest her soul—had been the type of lady who hadn't been bothered by convention and formalities. She'd been nothing but happy to allow her daughter to play with the daughter of a maid. And while there were obvious and inevitable differences in their educations and upbringing, the two girls hadn't allowed their stations in life to bother them much. When the time had come, Thea *insisted* upon taking Maggie as *her* lady's maid so they could remain together forever. But Maggie had never been as outgoing, adventurous, or as cocksure as Thea. Maggie was forever trying to talk Thea out of her latest foibles.

"I'm not actually *stealing* the horse," Thea qualified, poking an errant dark curl behind her ear. "He's *my* horse. Supposed to be at least." Thea held up her arms to allow Maggie to slip the day dress over her head.

"But didn't you say your brother lost the auction?" Maggie prompted, spinning Thea around so she could button the back of the gown. It was a routine they'd perfected over the years.

Maggie was short and blond with dark brown eyes and round cheeks. She had a constant smile on her pretty face, except for the times she was chasing Thea around to ensure she didn't end up in trouble. Those times Maggie usually had an exasperated expression on her face. This was certainly one of those times.

Thea rolled her eyes at her friend. "He did lose the auction, but that's hardly *my* fault. I gave Anthony specific instructions to win at all costs. If that blasted auction house would only allow females, *I* certainly wouldn't have lost."

Maggie arched a brow. "Perhaps your father gave Lord Anthony a limit. For his purse?" This was offered tentatively as if Maggie hated to bring it up, but thought it might be an important point.

"Oh, I'm certain he did," Theodora replied, "which is precisely why I intend to go in search of my father as soon as you finish buttoning me."

"Well, as to that, I'm finished now, milady," Maggie replied, patting Thea on the back to indicate that she was properly and completely buttoned.

Theodora swirled in a circle and spared a brief glance at herself in the looking glass. She'd never cared much about her appearance. She'd always been more interested in riding and horses than she'd ever been in frocks and the latest hair fripperies. She took in her own dark brown hair and deter-mined gray eyes. The gown was lovely. The *modiste* had just finished sewing it. It was a light peach satin with small flowers embroidered around the hem and sleeves. White stockings and gloves and matching peach beaded slippers completed her ensemble. She looked quite proper on the outside, even if she was seething with frustration on the inside.

Thea lifted her chin. "A pity I couldn't dress as a man and attend that auction. I swear I would have won."

Maggie sharply sucked in her breath and shook her head. "Oh, please don't say such things. Why, I'd have a fit if I had to dress you as a man. I'm a lady's maid, not a valet." She chuckled.

Thea smiled and lifted her shoulders while heaving a loud sigh. "Very well, I suppose this will have to do. Thank you for your help today, Mag. Wish me luck with Father."

"You're quite welcome," Maggie replied. "And I wish you all the luck in the world."

"I may need it." Thea swept her skirts into her hands, turned, and marched out the door of her bedchamber. Her destination was her father's study. Father wasn't often home. The Earl of Blackstone tended to spend most of his time in London with his mistress. Thea pushed the thought from her mind. It only served to anger her. Father was home this time of year because he came to visit the estate and see to the planning of their annual Christmastide ball. No doubt he'd be back to London as soon as he'd spoken to the housekeeper and butler. But for now, Thea had the perfect opportunity to ask her father about the horse auction. It was his fault the horse was at auction, after all.

She made her way through the wide upstairs corridor, then down the sweeping marble staircase that led to the foyer of her father's country house. Once downstairs, Thea continued through the foyer to another corridor that led to the far western edge of the estate where her father's study sat.

When she approached, the door to the study was open just a crack. Father liked to call at passersby upon occasion. Today, Theodora stuck her nose in the crack and blinked at the middle-aged man sitting behind the desk. Her father was tall and handsome, with a tinge of gray at the temples. Thea took after him in looks, or so Mother had always said. Thea certainly had inherited his dark hair and gray eyes. She hadn't taken after him in temperament, however. Perhaps that was why they'd rarely agreed upon anything.

"I see you, Miss." Her father's voice floated from the room. "And I'm quite certain I know why you've come."

Thea interpreted the comment for an invitation to enter the room. She pushed the door wide and strolled inside. "Good morning, Father," she said in her most pleasant tone. She and her father had never quite been on what one would call 'friendly' terms. He'd been gone to London much of her childhood, and just before her mother died, Thea had learned precisely what he'd been doing in London all those years. He was much more like a well-dressed stranger than a father to her. But at times she was forced to speak to him, and today was one of those times. She always strove to keep their interactions civil and quick.

Her father frowned. "I've been expecting your visit. Anthony returned last night and told me he lost the auction in London."

Thea marched over to stand in front of her father's wide mahogany desk. "That is precisely why I'm here," she allowed. "The Arabian was *my* horse."

Her father's frown intensified. "The Arabian was expensive, Theodora. You've no idea how much that horse ended up selling for."

Thea pressed her lips together. He'd called her Theodora. That just went to show how little her father knew her. He always called her Theodora. No one called her Theodora. Her mother and Anthony and Maggie and everyone called her Thea. As for what Father had said to her about the horse's price, she *wanted* to reply, "Then perhaps you should never have sold him to begin with so we wouldn't have to purchase him again." Instead, she said, "I told Anthony to use my dowry if necessary. The horse couldn't possibly have cost more than *that*," she replied in as calm a voice as she could muster, while utter frustration coursed through her veins.

Her father pushed himself back in his chair and narrowed his eyes on her. "First of all, there is no possible way I was going to approve of your dowry being spent on a horse, but what if I told you the horse cost the original amount we agreed to, *plus* your dowry, and double?"

Thea's mouth fell open. She couldn't help it. She quickly snapped it shut again before expelling a breath. "That cannot be. No Arabian has ever sold for *that* much."

"Trust me," Father replied. "That's the exact amount he went for. I was shocked to learn it myself. I'm confident Anthony did the best he could. He did not have my permission to pay anything near that amount."

"I cannot believe *anyone* would pay that much," Thea replied, resting her chin atop her thumb. She shook her head, trying to absorb the astonishing news. *Who* exactly would have paid such a price? It was outlandish. The Arabian was a gorgeous, nearly perfect piece of horseflesh indeed, but that amount of money was…ludicrous.

"My guess is the horse's relationship to the Duke of Harlowe had something to do with his price," Father continued.

Thea's brown knit into a frown. "The Duke of Har—"

Thea trailed off as Anthony stepped into the room. Her

brother stopped short as soon as he saw her. He gave her a wary look and took an unwitting step back.

"Come in, Anthony," Father said. "You might as well be a part of this discussion, too."

"I'm waiting to see if Thea intends to scratch out my eyes," Anthony said, a half-smile riding his lips. He resumed his saunter into the room, but continued to keep a watchful eye on Thea.

She crossed her arms over her chest and stared at her brother with one brow arched. "Father just told me how much the Arabian sold for."

Anthony let out a pent-up breath and sighed. "Believe me, I tried my best. I'd no idea anyone would bid *that* high."

"Are you certain you didn't mishear the cost?" Thea ventured.

Anthony's bark of laughter filled the room. He shook his head. "I may be five years your senior, but I am not yet old enough to be hard of hearing. I'm quite certain the Arabian sold for an exorbitant amount."

"Who would be foolish enough, reckless enough, to pay that much?" she demanded, her anger at her brother quickly finding a new target…the bastard who paid a fortune for *her* horse.

Anthony ran a hand across the back of his neck. "You don't understand, Thea. In addition to its bloodline, the horse belonged to the Duke of Harlowe. Everyone in the country has heard that sad story."

Thea gave her brother a patient smile. Of course she knew the story of the Duke of Harlowe. Or, more precisely, the *former* duke. Maggie loved to read Thea the society pages of the *Times* on a regular basis. The entire story had been chronicled there. After being purchased from her father six years ago, the Arabian had been the mount of the former duke's younger brother, a soldier who'd taken the steed to war. The poor young man had lost his life on the Continent and the magnificent horse had been carefully brought back to England by the Earl of Wellington himself to be returned to the Duke of Harlowe.

The horse could not replace his brother, of course, but the duke's younger brother had adored the animal and the steed was worth a small fortune—even before he'd been sold at auction for the mind-numbing amount Father had just reported.

The sad tale of the Duke of Harlowe did not end there, however. The young duke died unexpectedly in his sleep not two months after the horse's return. Because the duke had been unmarried and his younger brother was already dead, the man's title and all worldly possessions—including the horse—had been auctioned off by the soon-to-be new Duke of Harlowe. The new duke was a distant relation who'd arrived in London and caused nothing but scandal and havoc since his arrival. According to all sources, the man was a disgrace and the dowager duchess, the former duke's mother, who was still in mourning for both of her sons, was at her wits' end dealing with the shame the man was bringing upon the family name. Poor lady.

But the misfortunes of the Duke of Harlowe's kin were not Thea's concern. While she felt badly for the dowager duchess, and the unfortunate dead brothers, if someone was going to get that horse at auction, it might as well be her. He'd belonged to her previously, after all. And if her father wasn't such a selfish clod, he never would have sold the animal.

"I'm quite sorry for the Duke of Harlowe and his deceased brother, but I never wanted the horse because of the gossip surrounding its former owner," she insisted. No. She wanted the horse because of Mama. Riding was a passion that she and her mother had shared. Alabaster, the Arabian, had been the foal of Mama's horse, Helena. During the months her mother had laid dying in her bed, riding Alabaster had been Thea's only respite. She'd lost her mother, but she would *not* lose her horse. Only she *had* lost the horse, or more precisely, the horse had been ripped out from under her. Her father had wasted no time selling her mother's horse, and the Duke of Harlowe, who'd made the offer, had doubled it when he realized Thea's horse was descended from the same bloodline.

Father, ever one to make a profit, had sold both horses while Thea had been holding her mother's hand, ensuring that she drank at least a trickle of water, and sponging her heated body. Father hadn't cared. He'd barely come to visit Mama in all those months. Instead, he'd casually informed Thea via a *letter* of all things that her horse had been sold. Alabaster was gone before Thea even had a chance to make it to the stables to see him one last time.

She still shook with anger when she thought of it. At her mother's funeral, Thea had informed her father that she would never forgive him for his thoughtlessness. At the time, her father had attributed her reaction to her age of eighteen years and the fact that she was grieving her mother. "There are other horses in this world, Theodora," her father had blithely replied.

Now, four years later, and still unforgiven, her father had relented when Thea had pointed out that Alabaster was to be auctioned. She and Father had agreed upon a price and Thea had begged her brother to go to London and see that the matter was settled. She would finally have her beloved horse back. Only she wouldn't, because apparently someone had been mad enough to pay a ridiculous price for *her* horse.

"Harlowe's story may not have been of consequence to you," Anthony continued, "but the tragic story of the duke had every horse-loving man in London at Tattersall's that day with his pocketbook at the ready. I've never seen the place so crowded. It was madness."

Thea clenched her fists. Confound it. Why did her horse have to have former owners with such a dramatic history? She immediately chastised herself for having such an ungenerous thought. It was hardly the Duke of Harlowe's fault that he and his brother had died unceremoniously. But Thea hadn't counted on there being such stiff competition at the auction. And she certainly hadn't counted on the horse selling for more than Father had *in addition* to her dowry. There had to be a way to get more money and buy the horse from whoever had won the auction. Which reminded her...Anthony had yet to give her the name of her new sworn enemy.

"Who was it?" Thea demanded, plunking her fists to her hips and fighting the urge to stamp her slippered foot. "Who paid that much? Who won the auction?"

"Clayton." Anthony replied, inclining his head. "Viscount Clayton. I knew the man had money, but his investments must be doing even better than I'd heard."

"Indeed," Father added, nodding sagely.

"Clayton?" Theodora repeated, narrowing her eyes again. She tapped one finger against her cheek. "The name sounds vaguely familiar, but I'm not placing him."

"Viscount Clayton lives here in Devon. He's a good man. Smart. Shrewd. A favorite in Parliament. A scientist, I believe," Father said.

"Have I met him?" Thea asked, her eyes still narrowed. "I don't remember him. Does he attend our Christmastide ball?"

"I invite him to the ball every year, that's probably how you remember the name. But he always sends his regrets. He spends a great deal of time in London. He has been here before, but it's been many years. I'm certain you wouldn't

9

recall what a lot of old men were discussing. His family has lived at Clayton Manor for generations, of course. The current viscount is a force in Parliament from what I understand. Quite the politician. Knows everyone. Very connected."

Thea stepped toward the window and stared out toward the pasture. Perfect. An old man bought her horse. An old rich man. Someone who probably wouldn't even be able to ride the animal and enjoy it. Perhaps she could talk him out of it. Perhaps she could appeal to his kindness. He'd been in competition against other men at the auction. Perhaps a young woman could make him see reason, appeal to his softer side. At least he was a neighbor. She wouldn't have to travel terribly far to get Alabaster. Surely if she explained to Viscount Clayton that she didn't want the horse because of the notoriety surrounding his former owner, but because of her deep love of the animal, the man couldn't possibly refuse to sell her the horse. Not if he were a gentleman.

Thea turned swiftly to address Anthony and her father. "How far away is Lord Clayton's estate?"

"About an hour's ride from here," Father replied. "Due East."

Anthony narrowed his eyes on his sister. "Why are you asking?"

"I'm simply curious about the man," Thea replied, calmly folding her hands together in front of her. It wouldn't do for Anthony to guess that she intended to visit the viscount if she had to. Her brother would surely put a stop to it. Or try to at any rate.

Theodora turned once more and stared out the window, her mind racing. In addition to her dowry, she had additional monies that her mother had left her. Mother had left special instructions that she was to have control over it. It was meant to ensure that she would be able to pick her own husband, but instead, she would use that money and the additional amount to get her horse. A horse was more important than a husband after all. More loyal at least. Besides, what did Thea need with a dowry? She was already two and twenty and firmly on the shelf. Her mother's death prior to her come-out had ensured that Thea was able to skip that obnoxious event and then, two years later, when her father had *insisted* she arrive at the palace and be presented to the queen (her mother's childhood friend Lady Hophouse had sponsored her), Thea had promptly curtsied to the queen, made the obligatory rounds, and retreated to the countryside where she'd remained for the last two years, ignoring Lady Hophouse's repeated letters begging her to return to London and find a husband. Husbands weren't good for much. Horses were.

Of course even if her father gave her their originally agreed upon amount and she used her dowry *and* the additional money from her mother, it still wouldn't be enough to pay Viscount Clayton as much as he'd spent. How in the world would she come up with the difference? She wasn't entirely certain, but she knew the first step would be to write to the viscount and find out if an attempt to buy the horse from him would be in vain. She'd worry about how to procure the money later. Yes. She intended to write a letter to old, frail Lord Clayton, and appeal to the man's heart…the first chance she got.

# CHAPTER TWO

E
wan Fairchild, Viscount Clayton, stood just beyond the paddock gate behind his manor house watching his latest—and by far most extravagant—purchase run across the field. His newly hired horse trainer, Forrester, was there, ensuring the best of everything for the Arabian.

In his twenty-eight years of life, Ewan had never spent more on a purchase. Certainly not for a horse, not even for one of his London town houses, but the Arabian was magnificent, and irreplaceable as far as Ewan was concerned.

He hadn't intended to pay so much, of course. The price had been raised to a ridiculous extent by Lord Anthony Ballard, the son of the Earl of Blackstone. Ewan had never had a quarrel with Ballard. They were neighbors, in fact, but Ballard had seemed beyond intent upon winning the steed. It had surprised Ewan. He'd never known Ballard to be such a connoisseur of horseflesh. Was Ballard merely impressed by the animal's ancestry? Or was he just another one of the many who'd been intrigued by Harlowe's sad tale?

No, Ewan hadn't expected the bidding to go as high as it had, but in the end, he'd won and that was what mattered.

Ewan loved to win. Loved nothing better in fact. In Parliament, he excelled at winning by talking other gentlemen into seeing things his way. He had a knack for diplomacy and a reputation for being able to talk almost anyone into almost anything, but the auction hadn't required either of those skills. It had merely required the biggest pocketbook and luckily for Ewan, the years he'd spent investing his father's money since he'd inherited the title had paid off. In spades. As it turned out, in addition to his predilection for politics, he also had a knack for investment decisions. Besides, what was a bit of coin when a man's life hung in the balance?

Ewan prided himself on having all his affairs in order and winning every match he came up against, be it getting a bill passed in Parliament or a horse at auction. He had his entire life planned out to the slightest detail. He had a scientific mind and scientific minds liked to leave nothing to chance. Why, he even knew who he would marry, *not* that he intended to tie the parson's noose around his neck anytime soon. But one had to be prepared, and Ewan was always prepared. He'd chosen a future bride the same way he made all his decisions, with calculation and precision. Lord Malcolm was the leader of the opposition in Parliament, and a union between his family and Clayton's would go a long way toward solving many an argument in Whitehall. Malcolm's daughter, Lady Lydia, was twenty years old already, but apparently, she was in no hurry to marry either, or so her father claimed. Just as well. Ewan was hardly eager to marry a young girl. A union with Lydia would be just the advantageous match he'd always dreamed of. It would set up Ewan to be the de facto leader in Parliament. And that connection, along with his skills in diplomacy would be all he needed to ensure his bills were passed in a timely manner. The most important ones at least. The ones he truly cared about.

In addition to politics, friendship was one of the most important things in the world to Ewan. His own close friends were like brothers to him. He'd never had brothers of his own. He'd been an only child. When he'd met his close friends Kendall, Worth, and Bell at school, the lads had become thick as thieves in no time at all.

Of course Ewan had already known Phillip. Phillip was his oldest friend. They had met as small lads, no more than six years old. Phillip's father had been visiting Ewan's father and the two boys had hit it off immediately. They'd run down to the creek to try to float the small boat Ewan had just finished creating out of wood. What happened that day had changed the course of their lives. It was something Ewan would never forget, and something he would always be in Phillip's debt for.

None of Ewan's closest friends knew about his intent to wed Lady Lydia. No need to frighten them all before the time was right. They wouldn't be particularly surprised to learn that he would marry for politics, however. It's not as if any of them intended to marry for anything as crass as love. Well, Kendall perhaps, Ewan thought with a chuckle.

As far as Ewan was concerned, ambition was more important than love. Or at least it got you further in life.

Ewan glanced back toward the estate. His gaze lifted to a large second-floor window that faced that back of his land. Phillip's bedchamber. Phillip hadn't left that room for months. Phillip needed this horse. That was all there was to it.

Ewan strolled to the side of the paddock and his gaze traveled toward the front of the property where coach after coach arrived with the additional items he'd purchased at auction in London this week. He'd got nearly everything he'd gone to the city for, but the horse had been the most important item by far. Ewan and Forrester, the horse trainer, were going to ensure the Arabian did what he'd purchased him to do. They could not fail.

Ewan turned his gaze back to the horse. The stallion galloped past a small stable boy who flew backwards, upending a bucket of water he'd been carrying out to the far end of the paddock. Ewan jogged over and helped the boy to his feet.

"I'm sorry, me lord," the boy stumbled over his words, fear making his eyes bright. "Please forgive me, Sir. Don't send me off, please."

Ewan frowned. Why was this boy so frightened? "Are you the new boy Mr. Hereford just hired?"

I am, Sir," the boy gulped. "I began just two days ago. Please don't sack me, me lord. I won't make the mistake again, I promise."

"It was an honest mistake, Mr. ..." Ewan waited for the boy to provide him with a surname.

"Candle, me lord. Me name be Geoffrey Candle."

"Very well, Candle. As I was saying, it was an honest mistake and I do not terminate an honest man's employment over small trifles. In future, you may want to go the long way around near the fence to deliver the bucket."

Relief washed across the boy's face and the hint of a smile played across his cracked lips. "Aye, me lord. Certainly." He grabbed the bucket and was about to scurry back to the barn to refill it when Ewan stopped him again.

"Candle?" he called.

The boy turned back to face him, the bucket bumping against his leg. "Aye, me lord?"

Ewan pursed his lips. "Out of curiosity, where were you employed prior to coming here?"

"Lord Mayfeather's estate, me lord." The boy's face showed fear even before he shuddered.

"I see," Ewan replied. "Very well. That'll be all."

The boy scampered off and Ewan shook his head. Lord Mayfeather was an old man known for his temper. He lived on a dilapidated estate at least two hours ride away. He had a reputation for treating his servants poorly. No wonder the poor lad had been afraid of being sacked.

Ewan turned his attention back to the horse. The magnificent stallion tossed its mane and lifted its gorgeous hooves from the packed earth.

Phillip needed him. Ewan wouldn't fail his friend. After all, he owed him his life.

# CHAPTER THREE

The next afternoon, Thea squared her shoulders and expelled a long pent-up breath. She sat at the writing desk in the far corner of her bedchamber at the window. She'd never been much for writing letters, but she could certainly do an adequate job when the situation called for it. This time it called not just for writing, but for a bit of storytelling, perhaps. Not lying. No. No. Never that, but it didn't hurt to bend the truth if absolutely necessary. Now, did it?

She'd already crossed out several lines on a clean sheet of vellum before starting for a fifth time. She cleared her throat and read the words aloud as she wrote them.

*Dear Lord Clayton,*

*My brother tells me you won the auction for the Duke of Harlowe's Arabian. I would like to inquire as to whether you would be willing to sell the horse to me.*

*Blast.* No. That was simply boring. She crossed it out.

*Dear Lord Clayton,*

*It seems you and I have something in common. A love of fine horseflesh. Would you please sell the Arabian to me? I'd be ever so grateful.*

No. No. Far too desperate. She crossed it out.

*Dear Lord Clayton,*

*Allow me to introduce myself. My name is Lady Theodora Ballard. I am the daughter of the Earl of Blackstone and we are neighbors. I want your horse.*

Gah. Too blunt. More crossing out.

*Dear Lord Clayton,*

*You may not be aware, but Alabaster, the Arabian, was my horse when he was a foal. I've loved him since I was a child. My brother attempted to purchase him back for me last week, but it seems your desire to own the horse was as great as ours, greater in fact, as you were the winner of the auction. I appeal to you as a horse owner and lover. Will you please entertain an offer for me to purchase the horse from you for the full amount you paid? I would be ever so grateful. Besides, you must be regretting spending such an exorbitant amount.*

*Yours with sincerity,*
*Lady Theodora Ballard*

She read it over a few more times, settling on crossing out the very last line about regretting spending so much. That might just anger him.

"What do you think, Mag?" Thea said to the maid who was mending clothing on the other side of the room.

"Why didn't you mention how your father sold Alabaster without your knowledge?"

Thea contemplated the question for a moment. "Men like Viscount Clayton don't care about such things, Maggie. He's probably wanting his money back. I intend to give it to him."

Maggie shook her head. "I hope you know what you're doing and that spending that sort of money won't be something *you* regret one day."

Thea pursed her lips. "I only regret that dodgy old Viscount Clayton has forced me to spend so much to get what I want."

"There are other horses in the world, Thea," Maggie began.

"Don't you dare start," Thea said, giving her friend a look that indicated she wouldn't hear of it. "There is only one Alabaster and there only ever will be."

"Lord, you're stubborn," Maggie retorted, rolling her eyes. "Very well, send the letter. But I honestly have no idea how you think you'll come up with that much money."

Thea shrugged. She'd been thinking about that particular problem ever since she'd heard the amount Alabaster had sold for. "I've decided to write to my uncle Teddy. He's rich as Croesus and he loved my mother to distraction."

"Do you think he'll give you that much money?" Maggie wanted to know.

"I don't see why not. Besides, it shall only be a loan."

"A loan?" Maggie furrowed her brow.

"Yes. I will promise to repay him in future. It may take the rest of my life saving my pin money, of course, but I'll give it to him."

Maggie lowered her voice. Her eyes softened. She cleared her throat. "Thea, getting that horse back…it won't bring back your moth—"

"Don't," Thea warned, tears stinging the backs of her eyes. "I'm getting Alabaster back. No matter the cost."

Maggie averted her gaze, nodded, and returned her attention to her sewing.

THEA WAITED on tenterhooks for two entire torturous days before she received an answer from Viscount Clayton. She'd sent a footman directly to his estate with her letter, but his letter came back in the regular post as if he couldn't be bothered to believe it was of importance.

The moment her butler handed the letter to her, she ripped open the seal and scanned the page, all the while holding her breath as her heart pounded in her chest.

> *Dear Lady Theodora,*
>
> *While I appreciate your story and am sorry for your loss, I could not possibly part with the Arabian. I, too, have reasons for wanting him. He's a beautiful steed.*
>
> *Lord Ewan Fairchild, Viscount Clayton*

Thea read it once more. Then she turned over the page. It was blank. There had to be more to it. "That's it! That's all he has to say? He has 'reasons'? He didn't even bother to tell me what they are."

Maggie wrinkled her nose. "He's not required to tell you his reasons."

Thea fought the urge to crumple the letter in her fist. "You're right, but it would have been gentlemanly of him. I told him how much I love Alabaster." She was already pulling out a fresh piece of vellum to write back to the old curmudgeon.

> *Dear Lord Clayton,*

*While I appreciate that you may have your reasons for wanting Alabaster, though you failed to enumerate them, you cannot know what his loss has done to me. Please name your price. I eagerly await your reply.*

*Lady Theodora Ballard*

There, that was succinct enough, was it not? He couldn't possibly mistake that for some sort of coy negotiation tactic. She wanted that horse and was prepared to stop at nothing to get him.

This time, she had to wait even longer for the reply, prompting her to attempt to mount a trip to his estate more than once. Maggie had to talk her out of doing that, of course. Finally, the reply came one week later.

*Dear Lady Theodora,*

*It is with deep regret that I must inform you that nothing and no price could entice me to part with Alabaster. As I'm certain you're aware, he's an incomparable horse. I commend you on your knowledge of horseflesh.*

Red flashed before Thea's eyes. She crumpled the letter in her hands, her face heating with undiluted anger. How dare he refuse her and how dare he patronize her while refusing her!

Maggie hurried into the room. "What did he say this time?"

"He refused my offer," Thea said through clenched teeth.

Maggie cocked her head to the side. "I don't understand. Didn't you ask him to name his price?"

"I did!" Thea replied, indignation filling her.

Mag's face fell. "I'm terribly sorry, Thea. If he refused that offer, he's clearly intent upon keeping the horse."

Thea's nostrils flared. She glared at the odious letter sitting atop her desk. She would not write to him again. The hideous man had left her no choice. If she were staring him in the eye, he couldn't refuse her so easily. She would simply have to pay him a visit.

# CHAPTER FOUR

**E**wan sat behind the desk in his study, intent upon his conversation with Mr. Forrester, who sat in the chair facing him on the other side of the desk. Both men were enjoying a brandy.

"It's true, my lord," Forrester said. "I've been studying it extensively for years. There is definite scientific evidence that working with animals can cure certain illnesses, including illnesses of the mind. It improves the mental state and can lessen worry and disquiet. The practice was recorded as far back as Roman times. It's been documented extensively."

"Precisely why I wanted to work with you, Forrester," Ewan said, leaning back in his chair.

"Specifically, I've worked with men who've suffered extreme shocks to their mental states. Just as you've described your friend," Forrester continued.

"Yes, well. It won't be a simple task to convince him to begin the treatment," Ewan replied. "Phillip hasn't spoken a word since he came to live with me last summer."

"From what I understand, that's not uncommon, my lord."

"This horse is my last resort. I'm hoping Phillip will respond well."

"The Arabian is in perfect condition, my lord. Whoever's had him since he left Portugal has done an excellent job with his care."

"I'm glad to hear that at least. I hope to begin—" A knock at the door interrupted Ewan's thought. He glanced up to see Humbolt, the butler standing there.

The butler cleared his throat. "Apologies for the interruption, my lord, but you have a visitor."

Ewan frowned. "A visitor?" He wasn't expecting anyone, and people rarely visited the countryside in the autumn unless invited to a hunting party or something similar. "Who is it, Mr. Humbolt?"

The butler's shoulders drew up and he lowered his gaze. "It's a…er…young lady, my lord."

Ewan's frown intensified. "A young lady?" he echoed. "Is she alone?"

"She is, my lord," Humbolt replied. The servant glanced surreptitiously at Mr. Forrester as if he regretted admitting the somewhat scandalous news in front of the man.

Ewan cocked his head to the side. Who could it possibly be? He didn't know many young ladies in the area and the ones he did weren't likely to pay him a visit. He'd never been one for affairs or mistresses, either. All the young ladies he knew were in London, including his soon-to-be betrothed, Lydia. She wouldn't have come this far to visit and certainly not by herself.

Forrester made as if to stand. "I can go, my lord."

"No," Ewan replied, almost too forcefully. "That is to say, I'd like to continue our talk, Forrester." He turned his attention back to the butler. "Did the young lady give a name, Mr. Humbolt?"

24

The butler gave Mr. Forrester another nervous glance. "She says her name is Lady Theodora Ballard, my lord."

Ballard. The name was immediately familiar. Ewan had just received a series of letters from the young woman. She wanted to purchase the Arabian. He'd written back quite clearly refusing and wishing her well. Apparently, she wasn't one to take no for an answer. He'd never expected her to arrive on his doorstep, however. This was bothersome.

"You say she's alone, Humbolt?" Ewan clarified.

The butler cleared his throat once more. "A maid accompanied her, my lord, but that young woman appears to be waiting in the carriage for her mistress."

How curious. Ewan scratched at his jaw. He'd actually done a bit of research on the girl. She was Lord Anthony Ballard's sister. Unmarried as far as Ewan was aware. Unmarried and on the shelf if the rumors he uncovered were to be believed. Apparently, she hoped her arrival on his doorstep would cause him to change his mind about selling the horse. First, she was sorely mistaken. He would never change his mind. Second, he didn't have time to deal with a spoiled spinster who wouldn't take no for an answer. A bit of anger flared in his chest.

Ewan sighed. "Please tell Lady Theodora that I am otherwise occupied."

"Are you certain, my lord?" Humbolt asked, his gray eyebrow arching.

"Are you questioning my decision, Humbolt?" Ewan frowned again. It was quite unlike Humbolt not to immediately carry out his orders.

Humbolt's face flushed. "Not at all, my lord. It's just that…" He straightened his shoulders, clearly searching for the correct words to use. "She seems the sort who won't leave readily, my lord."

This time Ewan arched a brow. "If she refuses to leave,

Humbolt, alert me immediately. I'll ensure she goes." His jaw was tight.

"As you wish, my lord." Humbolt bowed and retreated from the room.

Ewan returned his attention to the horse trainer. "My apologies for the interruption, Forrester. Now, where were we?"

But as the man spoke, Ewan's mind wandered back to his conversation with Humbolt and the letters he'd exchanged with Lady Theodora Ballard. Ewan had got the distinct impression from her letters that she would not be happy with his refusal to sell the horse. He'd also considered how much she must want the horse if she'd been willing to pay the exorbitant amount that he'd paid for it. Her brother had obviously been betting on the horse for his sister. But if Ballard had had the money, why hadn't he won the auction? Ewan had just assumed the price had gone too high for the son of the earl. Something about the entire situation didn't seem right.

Ewan could well understand Lady Theodora's disappointment, but he had no intention of selling the horse to her. And it wouldn't do for her reputation for him to entertain her alone either. He was doing her a favor by refusing to take her call. Besides, he could just imagine the chit crying and begging him to sell the horse to her. He wasn't about to have to share his handkerchief and be subjected to such dramatics. No, much better to send her along her way without the hope that he might someday relent.

As Forrester continued to speak, however, Ewan couldn't seem to banish the matter from his mind. The young woman clearly was overly confident, or she wouldn't have arrived on his doorstep unannounced after he'd been clear in his letters that he had no intention of selling the Arabian.

"And so, you see, my lord, I think we have as good a

chance as any with the treatment," Forrester was saying when Ewan began to listen again.

"Good, good," Ewan replied absently, while the picture of what Lady Theodora Ballard must look like played through his imagination. She was a spinster so no doubt she was homely, or perhaps it was a strident personality that had prevented her from finding a match. He vaguely remembered seeing her at her father's estate years ago, but she'd merely been a girl then. He had hardly any memory of the chit.

Mr. Forrester continued to speak as Ewan shifted in his chair. *Blast.* Why couldn't he stop thinking about the audacity of the young woman who was even now being ejected from his drawing room?

As if his body was acting separately from his mind, Ewan stood. "Excuse me for a moment, Forrester. I'll return shortly."

Ewan took ground-devouring strides toward the drawing room. He told himself the entire time that if she were already gone, he would *not* go out to the drive to see if he could catch a glimpse of her. After all, he had no intention of rewarding her rude behavior by taking her call. No. He just wanted to...see her. For some reason, he felt an overwhelming desire to put a face with her name. He told himself it was in order to know if he ever encountered her in the future, whether in town at the market or even back in London. He needed to know who he'd refused and turned away in case they were ever to meet face-to-face again.

As he approached the door of the drawing room, Ewan let out a pent-up breath he hadn't even realized he'd been holding as he heard Humbolt speaking in a loud, clear voice. "Be that as it may, my lady, Viscount Clayton was quite clear that he is unable to take your call."

"Did you tell him how far I've traveled?" a distinctly piqued female voice replied sharply.

Ewan lifted his brows. Just as Humbolt had said, this young woman clearly wasn't leaving without some resistance. Normally, such audacity would have earned her a swift visit from him and some harsh words as he escorted her to the door, but now it only served to make him more curious to see her face.

"I told the viscount your name, my lady. I've no idea if he's aware of your address," Humbolt was saying.

Ewan strode up to the door and, remaining at least two steps away, peered inside the crack that Humbolt had left.

She stood in front of the settee. She wore a matching pelisse over a gown of light green. Long white gloves, small leather traveling boots, and a bonnet of the latest fashion with a wide green ribbon tied beneath her chin. She was slender and tall, and her hair was dark and swept beneath the hat. Her profile revealed a pretty enough face, but it wasn't until she turned toward the door, with narrowed eyes, that he saw the glint of steel in the gray of her eyes. She was absolutely stunning. There was no other way to describe her. Stunning, and angry, with one of the most determinedly set jaws he'd ever seen on a female. No wonder Humbolt had been worried she wouldn't leave quietly. There was clearly nothing quiet about this woman.

Those steel-gray eyes flashed with fire as if a blacksmith had struck an anvil and made a spark deep within them. Ewan watched her carefully. She might be gorgeous, but he had no intention of selling the horse to her or anyone.

"Well, I'm sorry to say that's not good enough for me, Mr. Humbolt," came the young lady's overly confident, self-assured voice. "I have no intention of leaving until I've spoken to the viscount."

Humbolt's voice replied firm and calm. "I'm sorry, my lady, but that is quite impossible—"

"I'll wait," the lady replied sharply and plopped back down upon the settee, settling her gloved hands into her lap.

That was it. This could not stand. Ewan kicked open the door with the toe of his boot and stepped inside.

"Not entirely impossible, Humbolt. Here I am, and I have a few things I'd like to say to our *guest*."

## CHAPTER FIVE

When Ewan stepped into the room, his gaze locked with Lady Theodora's. Anger flashed in her eyes, but there was something else there, too. *Triumph.* Given his presence she no doubt believed she'd won.

"My lord," Humbolt said as he bowed and took his leave. Ewan knew the man would not go far in the event Ewan required his assistance.

Lady Theodora gave the butler a tight (but still triumphant) smile on his way out.

Ewan set his jaw, but remembered his manners. "My lady." His tone was hardly pleasant, but he managed a gentlemanly bow. "It's been many years. A pleasure to see you again."

They both knew the 'pleasure' bit was a lie, but manners were manners.

She lifted her chin. "*Unfortunately*, I don't recall our first meeting, my lord. Thank you for the *honor* of your time." Sarcasm dripped from her lips.

"As I'm certain Mr. Humbolt informed you, I'm otherwise

occupied with a guest in another room. What can I do to help you, my lady?" His smile was tight and fake.

She looked momentarily flustered as if she hadn't expected to get this far and therefore wasn't entirely prepared for what she intended to say next. But her dismay was quickly replaced with a gleam in her eyes, a gleam that made Ewan immediately wary.

She folded her hands together in front of her. Her matching green reticule, which he'd previously missed, swung from her wrist. She wasted no time getting precisely to her point. "I would like to purchase Harlowe's Arabian from you."

He pressed his lips together tightly before replying. "I am aware. The answer is no."

Frustration flittered across her pretty face. "May we not discuss it?" He could tell she was doing her best to sound friendly. He could almost laugh at her poor attempt. He would laugh, in fact, if he wasn't so angry that she was wasting his time.

Ewan clasped his hands together behind his back. "There's nothing to discuss. I thought I made myself clear in my last letter. I regret that you wasted your time traveling here."

She lifted her chin even higher. "I came here to discuss the terms."

He clenched his jaw. By God, this woman was stubborn. "There will be no terms. The Arabian is not for sale. Now if you'll just—" He turned to escort her toward the door.

"He's *my* horse." Her harsh voice seemed to crack against the walls of the room.

Ewan turned back toward her and gave her a patient smile. "On the contrary, he's mine."

She pulled so tightly on the strings to her reticule that Ewan was certain they would snap. "Why do you refuse to bargain?" she asked, doing her best to attempt a smile again. "You haven't even heard my offer yet."

Ewan crossed his arms over his chest and tilted his head to the side. He regarded her down the side of his nose. There was something commanding about this young woman's presence. Something that made him want to hear what she said next. Even if the answer would always be *no*.

"I hope you don't mind me asking," he began, "but why is it that *you're* here to discuss the matter of the horse's sale, instead of say, your brother or your father?"

"I do mind you asking," she replied, blinking her long dark eyelashes at him. That false smile was still pinned to her face. "But the answer is, if I want something done correctly, I do it myself."

"Is that so?" Ewan asked. No wonder the chit was still on the shelf. What sane man would want to deal with her demands and waspish temper?

"Indeed," she replied, inclining her head to the side. "If I'd been allowed in that auction house to begin with the horse would already be mine."

Ewan continued to watch her. He'd never known a young lady to be so certain of herself or so aggressive. Most of the young ladies of his acquaintance simpered and giggled into their handkerchiefs and feigned fainting. He was positive Lady Theodora hadn't fainted once in her life. He had to know. "Lady Theodora, may I ask you a question?"

"Certainly," she replied, her shoulders relaxing a hint. He could tell she was still trying to seem friendly in the hopes that he might still sell her the horse. She was sorely mistaken, but he'd take the false niceties as long as he could get them.

"Have you ever...fainted?" He narrowed his eyes on her.

She drew up her shoulders tight again. "Certainly not. Fainting is for simpering nitwits."

He nodded, doing his best to hide his smile. "Somehow I knew you would say that."

"Allow me to keep you from wasting anymore of your precious time, my lord, or mine," she said next. She took a deep breath and her nostrils flared. "I know how much you paid for the horse. Surely you have regrets."

His brows shot up. Well, *that* comment had certainly been direct. "Not one, actually," he replied, grinning at her. He didn't know what her game was, but she certainly wasn't about to win her argument by telling him he'd been a fool for paying so much for the Arabian.

She narrowed her eyes on him. "No one's has *ever* paid that much for a horse."

"They have now," he replied simply.

"Even Pegasus, the son descended directly from of one of the original Godolphin Arabians didn't sell for that much at Tattersall's two years ago," she pointed out, crossing her arms over her chest.

"I know," he replied, still eyeing her carefully. "My friend, the Duke of Worthington purchased him. You seem to know quite a lot about horses and their prices."

"Believe me, I do," she replied. "I've studied the subject extensively. I've had my eye on the papers and auction prices for years. Ever since Alabaster was stolen from me."

"Stolen?" Ewan's brows shot up once again. "I hadn't heard the horse had ever been stolen."

She cleared her throat. "Well, perhaps he wasn't precisely *stolen*, but my father took him from me and sold him to the Duke of Harlowe without my consent four years ago."

Ewan refrained from pointing out that any horse of hers was hers at her father's discretion. They both knew it. There was little need to say it. "I'm sorry to hear that," he said instead. "He's a fine horse. But allow me not to waste anymore of *your* precious time, my lady. I have no intention of selling the Arabian. There is no amount of money that would sway my decision."

Her jaw momentarily dropped open. "What? Why, that's unreasonable."

Another patient smile. "I prefer to call it decisive."

Panic sparked in her eyes. She glanced wildly around the room before saying, "What if I offered you double?"

Ewan arched a brow. "Double? Double what I paid at auction? Are you quite certain you're aware of the amount?"

Her eyes narrowed nearly to slits. "I'm not an imbecile or a child, my lord. I'm quite aware of the purchase price and I know the value of coin."

Ewan pressed his lips together to keep from smiling. She had spunk, this young lady. He had to give her that much. She didn't appear to be afraid of anyone or anything and she certainly knew precisely what she wanted. "Forgive me for asking, my lady, but are you currently in possession of that amount of money?"

More panic flashed through her expressive eyes. "Not at the moment," she admitted, clutching her reticule. "But I'm entirely capable of procuring that amount. I'll just need a bit of time."

Ewan shook his head and took a step toward the door. He'd entertained this nonsense long enough. If Anthony Ballard or his father were willing to pay anything close to the amount she was offering, Ewan would have lost the auction. Double was a ludicrous amount of money. Furthermore, Lady Theodora obviously wasn't a skilled negotiator if she was starting her bid at double. The last thing Ewan wanted to do was to take advantage of his neighbor Lord Blackstone's daughter. "I'm afraid not, my lady. Though I do appreciate your eye for horseflesh. The horse is not for sale at any price. Too bad I cannot take you with me the next time I go to the auction house. I honestly wouldn't want to bid against you." He opened the door wide and gestured for her to walk through it. "Now, if you'll excuse me, I have a busy afternoon. I'll have Humbolt show you out." Ewan turned to leave, but had only taken one step when her loud voice stopped him.

"Are you *mad*?"

He stopped and turned back to face her. "My lady?"

"You'd refuse *twice* the purchase price?" Her chest was heaving, and her eyes were flashing gray fire at him. She was quite magnificent really. Too bad she was infuriating.

Ewan reminded himself to take a long deep breath. He was used to being in heated negotiations in Parliament and he'd learned long ago that the coolest head usually prevailed. Why this young woman made him lose his infamous cool was anyone's guess.

He lifted both brows and regarded her down the length of his nose. "I am not mad, my lady," he replied. "Some things are simply not for sale."

"Fine." She was nearly shaking with rage, but she managed to say in a relatively calm voice, "May I at least *see* the Arabian, my lord?"

Ewan eyed her for a few seconds before the word slipped from his lips. Simple. Calm. Unheated. "No."

"No?" Her eyes went round with surprise. Her mouth was tight. More fire flashed in her steely eyes as they narrowed on him. Her nostrils flared again. "May I ask why?"

"You may ask," Ewan replied, "but I fear you may not like the answer."

"Try me, my lord." Her arms were tightly crossed over her chest once more.

"Very well, Lady Theodora. The truth is that I have the distinct impression that you've never heard the word 'no' before in your life. And I am of the belief that you would do well to hear it for once." He said every word calmly, without raising his voice, but by the end of his diatribe, he was most certainly trembling with anger.

Lady Theodora bent her head and she stared at the floor silently for what felt like minutes but what was probably no more than a few seconds. For one awful moment, he wondered if he'd gone too far. He was a gentleman after all, and she was a young, unmarried lady, his neighbor. The chit's rudeness had taken him off guard, but had he been *too* ungentlemanly? Had he said too much? Was the young woman about to burst into tears in his drawing room? Was she already crying? Lady Lydia had burst into tears once over something he'd said that had been far less direct. It seemed to him that young ladies were often wont to burst into tears over simple matters.

Ewan watched Lady Theodora warily. She lifted her head, drew up her shoulders, pursed her lips, and grabbed up her skirts. Her eyes were quite devoid of any tears as she said, "Very well. If we are going to tell each other what we believe the other needs to hear…" Venom dripped from her voice as she strode past him toward the door and pushed it wide so violently it cracked against the far wall in the corridor. She turned to face him, "You, Viscount Clayton, are the very definition of an ass."

Then, she turned sharply on her heel. The clip of her boots on the marble floor rang out as she made her way across the foyer and to the front door, which Humbolt had already deftly opened for her.

Ewan watched her go with a half-bemused smile on his lips. How in the devil's name had it come to this? In Parliament, he was known for his friendliness and diplomacy, but he'd certainly just made a solid enemy in Lady Theodora Ballard. He shook his head. Not that the chit had given him much of a choice. The girl was beautiful and presumably well-bred, but she was a complete shrew if her performance in his drawing room just now was anything to judge her behavior on. Any flicker of guilt he felt for refusing to allow her to see the horse was quickly replaced by anger when he thought of some of the outrageous things she'd said to him. The girl was clearly selfish. She might be good-looking, but beauty meant little when paired with a waspish temper.

First, she'd written him, then she'd come to visit without an invitation. Ewan turned and sauntered back toward the study to resume his discussion with Forrester, but all the while he couldn't dismiss the feeling that he hadn't seen the last of Lady Theodora Ballard.

CHAPTER SIX

"That no good, lecherous, old goat!" Thea nearly shouted as the door to her father's coach shut behind her. One of Viscount Clayton's footmen had just helped her inside the conveyance from the gravel drive in front of the manor house.

Maggie, who sat on the opposite seat, let her needlework drop into her lap. She winced. "Oh, no. That must mean it didn't go well."

"It did not," Thea allowed. She was still breathing so heavily through her nostrils she was practically snorting. She distracted herself by arranging her skirts upon the burgundy velvet-tufted seat while the coachman set the vehicle into motion back toward her father's estate.

"He's hideous," Thea added, pulling her reticule from her wrist and tossing it upon the seat next to her. "He's contemptible. Odious."

"You mentioned he's a lecherous old goat," Maggie said in an entirely even tone. The maid had already gathered up her needlework and was back at it. "Was he quite elderly, then?" she asked casually.

"No, actually," Thea unhappily allowed. She scrunched up her face and glared out the window. "He was quite a bit younger than Father had led me to believe. Couldn't have been much past thirty years old."

"Is that so?" Maggie replied, not even glancing up from her needlework. Maggie had been through a score of dramas with Thea and had learned to take them all in stride. Clearly her friend didn't realize how very serious *this* drama was. "Was he handsome?"

Thea's jaw dropped. "Handsome? Why, I just told you how odious he is. Why would you ask if he's handsome?" she grumbled.

Maggie shrugged. "I assumed you meant he's odious because he refused to sell you the horse, not because of his countenance."

"He *did* refuse to sell me the horse. The man is hideous!" Thea declared, absently smoothing her hands over her skirts.

"Hideous or odious?" Maggie asked as she pulled the needle through the cloth.

Thea snorted again. "Both!"

"Very well, but was he handsome or not?" Maggie prodded.

Thea crossed her gloved arms sharply across her chest and glared at her friend for a moment while she contemplated the question. It made her even more angry to admit even to herself, but the fact was that the man *was* handsome, blast it all. When he'd first entered the room, she'd assumed he was a steward or some other servant sent to send her away, but when she'd realized he was Viscount Clayton himself, she'd been somewhat taken aback by his looks. Of course she hadn't allowed herself to show it, as she'd been entirely distracted by the fight she was primed to have with him, but the man was tall, blond, and slim with the most heavenly lidded blue eyes she'd ever seen. They'd looked at her as if they'd known all her secrets and they carried a shrewd wisdom that told her that her normal theatrics were not about to work on him. She'd tried them at any rate. Tried and failed.

"What does it matter if he's handsome or not?" Thea shot back, thoroughly annoyed with Maggie for even asking something as inconsequential as the man's looks.

A sly smile spread across Maggie's face. "Oh, that means he *is* handsome." The maid nodded knowingly.

*Blast it.* Maggie knew her too well. The maid could tell by Thea's refusal to answer that the answer was yes. "Being handsome doesn't negate the fact that he's odious," Thea insisted, lifting her nose into the air. She stared out the coach's window into the brightly colored autumn trees as the carriage rumbled further and further away from her beloved Alabaster.

"Very well," Maggie replied, still attending to her needle-work. "What did the odious man say?"

Thea took a deep breath. "Not only did he refuse to sell him to me, he refused even to allow me to *see* him."

Maggie lifted her brows. "Well, that does seem odious of him. What did you say to him to make him so set against you?"

Thea pressed her lips together and wrinkled up her nose. "Why do you think this is my fault? Perhaps he's just odious."

Maggie glanced up from her needlework long enough to give Thea a highly skeptical look. "Shall I remind you that I know you well enough to know that whatever words were exchanged between yourself and Viscount Clayton, yours *had* to be provoking. Provoking enough to see you expelled from the house without so much as a visit to the horse."

Thea shifted uncomfortably in her seat. As usual, Mag was right. Thea had to unhappily admit to herself that *she* was to blame for angering the man to the point that he'd refused to allow her access to Alabaster. Why had she allowed the viscount's callous refusal to negotiate to make her lose her temper?

"Never in my life have I experienced such a vehement dislike of someone upon first meeting him," Thea declared.

Maggie sighed. "You still haven't answered my question. What did you say to him to make him so angry?"

Thea frowned, but there was no use lying to Mag. "Very well. I may have asked him if he were mad."

Maggie's jaw dropped open. "You didn't!"

"He was being entirely unreasonable," Thea retorted. "I have every reason to believe he's insane."

Maggie closed her mouth and shook her head. "Because he didn't want to sell you a horse he purchased fairly at auction? That is his prerogative."

"But I offered him *double*," Thea replied, as if that bit of news should explain away the entire ordeal.

Maggie's eyes went wide as moons. "Double? Double what?"

"Double the price he paid at auction." Thea turned her head away. She couldn't watch the judgement in Maggie's eyes as she admitted her folly.

Maggie's voice was an incredulous whisper. "You don't have that sort of money."

Thea traced a finger along the bottom of the window. "*I* know that, but he doesn't. What sort of a madman would refuse that amount of money?" She dared a glance at the maid.

Maggie pinched the bridge of her nose and closed her eyes as if she were experiencing a headache. "So, you called him mad, and he asked you to leave?"

Thea nodded slowly. "I called him mad and then asked to see Alabaster and *then* he asked me to leave. But not before displaying the unmitigated gall to tell me that he believed I'd

41

never heard the word 'no,' before and I was sorely in need of it."

A bark of laughter escaped Maggie's lips and she clapped a gloved hand over her mouth. "He didn't," she said in an amazed half-whisper.

Thea rolled her eyes. "Yes. He did."

Maggie moved closer to the edge of her seat. "What did you say in reply? I can only imagine how pert it was."

Thea winced and shrugged. "I called him an ass and then I left."

Maggie's hand flew to her mouth again, this time in obvious shock. "Oh, good heavens. Of course you did."

"He *is* an ass," Thea maintained, her leg bouncing up and down beneath her skirts.

"Perhaps, but you know you should not have allowed him to rile you so much that you called him that, Thea." Maggie's gaze captured hers.

Thea winced. Maggie rarely called her by her first name. She was being rebuked indeed. And she deserved it. She knew. Thea wasn't proud of the fact that she'd allowed Viscount Clayton to make her so angry she'd reacted in such an unladylike manner. The look Maggie was giving her didn't require additional words. Thea and her friend were both thinking the same thing, Thea's mother would never have approved of her only daughter behaving in such a wild manner. It didn't even matter that she'd behaved that way in front of a neighbor and a peer. Mama wouldn't have countenanced Thea behaving in that manner in front of the lowliest servant either. She hadn't raised her daughter to be a rude termagant. Thea closed her eyes as shame washed over her.

"You'd better hope the viscount doesn't pay your father a visit and tell him about your behavior," Maggie added.

Thea slumped down in her seat and crossed her arms tightly over her middle, contemplating the whole awful situation. She may have behaved like a petulant schoolgirl, but she still wanted to see Alabaster. Desperately.

"I hadn't contemplated that," Thea replied, misery washing over her.

"Don't fret over it too much," Maggie replied, leaning over and patting Thea on the knee. "I suspect Lord Clayton is merely happy to be rid of you."

"He's not rid of me yet," Thea replied.

"What do you mean?" Maggie gave her an extraordinarily wary look.

"I don't care whether Lord Clayton refused to allow me to see Alabaster. He's *my* horse and I'm not about to let that man stop me from paying him a visit."

Maggie was shaking her head. "What do you intend to do?"

"I intend to… I intend to…" Thea glanced out the window of the carriage and saw a stableboy running up a nearby lane. An idea flashed through her mind. A mad idea. But one that just might work. "I intend to ask you to make me boy's clothes. I'll need breeches and a neckcloth and—"

"Breeches?" Maggie's eyes widened until they looked like moons. "And a boy's shirt?"

"Yes," Thea replied with a decided nod. "I'll need both. Oh, and a cap too. To hide my hair."

Maggie closed her eyes and swallowed. "I certain I'll regret asking this, milady, but why exactly do you need such clothing?"

Thea turned and gave her friend a half-wild smile. She could pass for a boy, at least temporarily. "Because I intend to become a lad, Maggie. At least long enough to see my horse."

## CHAPTER SEVEN

E wan's slight knock on the bedchamber door was met by silence. It was always met by silence. He waited a few moments before turning the handle and pushing it open.

The maid had come in as she did each morning to open the curtains and allow light to stream through the large glass windows that covered the wall on the far side of the room.

Ewan allowed his eyes to adjust to the brightness for a few moments before his gaze fell on his friend, sitting in a chair in the corner, facing the opposite wall.

Phillip's location around the room each day often varied, but the fact that he sat in silence, did not.

"Good morning," Ewan offered as he closed the door behind himself and moved farther into the room.

More silence met his ears.

"A beautiful day today," Ewan continued. Outside the window the trees were filled with beautiful bright autumn colors. The entire landscape looked as if it was set ablaze. It was one of Ewan's favorite times of year. Phillip rarely looked out the window.

"How are you feeling?" Ewan asked. He asked the same question every morning even though he knew he would receive no answer.

"I've seen to my books after an early meeting with my solicitor and this afternoon I intend to go riding," Ewan continued, talking only to himself.

It was awkward, carrying on a one-sided conversation, but that is what the doctors had told him to do. *Act as if nothing is different, my lord. When he is ready, he will reply.*

Ewan hoped they were correct. But with every passing day, with no response from Phillip, a bit of hope faded.

They'd been friends since they were lads. Their fathers had been as close as brothers. They'd done everything together. Learned to ride, learned to hunt, learned to swim. It had been during a swimming expedition when they were but seven years old that Phillip had shown himself to be the most loyal of friends.

They'd begun the day fishing in a lake on Phillip's father's property. The fishing expedition had turned into an afternoon of swimming under the hot sun. Ewan and Phillip had each been diving and holding their breath. Even as a child, Ewan's competitive nature had got the best of him. He had to be the one to hold his breath the longest and win. Only he'd dived too deep in an effort to stay under longer and ended up getting his clothing caught on the branch of a tree that had fallen in the water.

Apparently, Phillip had realized that his friend had been underwater too long and had come after Ewan, ripping at the branch, his own hands bloody and torn by the time it was over. Ewan didn't remember much after.

Phillip had grabbed him beneath the arm and swam him back to shore where he pushed water out of Ewan's lungs. Ewan was coughing up the last of it and regaining consciousness when their fathers had ridden up on horseback, alerted by Phillip's shouts.

His friend had saved his life that day and Ewan had vowed to return the favor if ever he were called upon. Only Ewan hadn't gone to war as Phillip had. As a viscount, Ewan wasn't in the Army. Instead, he did what he could for the cause of the war and the soldiers from his place in Parliament. Phillip didn't have a title. He took a position as an officer in the Army and was sent to the Continent.

He'd been wounded in the war, shot in the shoulder and fallen from his horse. They'd found him still alive when combing a battlefield days after the battle. He'd been taken back to a medical camp and eventually returned to England.

Ewan hadn't been there the day his friend needed him. He hadn't been by his side on the battlefields of Europe, but the moment Ewan had heard that Phillip was injured, Ewan had gone to Dover and met his ship. He'd brought an extra coach fitted comfortably for an invalid, but when he'd seen Phillip disembark, Ewan realized that it wasn't his friend's body that was broken. Phillip may have been thinner and paler, but it was his mind that was broken. The man could walk, his bruises and broken bones had healed, but he didn't say a word that day and he hadn't spoken since.

Ewan spent several more minutes in his friend's room recounting boring little tidbits about the estate and some things he'd read in the paper before standing to take his leave. This is how their conversations went every day. Entirely one-sided. But Ewan dutifully arrived and made the effort no matter what. He would not let his friend down.

Ewan passed by the window. He stopped in front of the glass panes and looked down into the paddock where Forrester and one of the stablehands were working with Alabaster. He wished he could show Phillip the horse, but after many long talks with Mr. Forrester, they'd agreed that

Phillip needed to be a bit stronger before they would tell him about Alabaster.

Moments later, Ewan left Phillip's room feeling less hopeful about his friend's condition than he had in weeks. Phillip still wouldn't speak. He still wouldn't leave his rooms. How in the world would Ewan ever convince him to come out to the stables and ride?

Ewan had spent a small fortune on Alabaster. Had he even done the right thing? Would Alabaster truly be able to help Phillip regain what he had lost? Or was Phillip's injury more physical than mental? Only time would tell. There was still one thing about Phillip that he knew and that was that the man harbored a secret in his very identity. No one could know he was here.

## CHAPTER EIGHT

Thea pulled the cap down tightly over her brow before alighting from the small pony she'd ridden through the night to Lord Clayton's estate. Thank heavens there was a full moon tonight or she would have been entirely in darkness.

Maggie was the only person who knew where Thea had gone. They'd quarreled at great length both over Thea's intention to sneak into Clayton's stables and over Thea's insistence upon riding to Lord Clayton's estate alone. At night. In the dark. Dressed as a lad, no less.

But in the end Thea had stubbornly insisted upon her plan. "It makes no sense to take a coach. Why would a lad arrive in a coach? I must be alone and take a pony."

Of course, Maggie had asked Thea a variety of perfectly reasonable additional questions such as: What if you're caught? What if you're *shot*? And the maid had ended her lecture with the warning, "If you are caught or shot, it will be no more than you deserve."

"You let me worry about that," had been Thea's defiant reply, but now that she was on Clayton's property, a good bit of apprehension had somehow managed to sneak its way into her mind, making her doubt herself. She shook her head and adjusted the dark cap she was wearing. She'd come this far. She would see it through.

Maggie had spent the better part of the last sennight busily sewing the clothing for Thea's clandestine journey.

After the clothing was finished, Thea had waited another few days for the moon to be full enough to ride by. The entire plot was dangerous and risky, but nothing was going to keep her from seeing her horse.

She slipped off the pony and tied him to a nearby tree. She'd spent a great deal of time researching Lord Clayton's estate. To her delight, she'd found a map of the area in her father's library. The bits that weren't outlined there, she'd filled in by paying a visit to another neighbor, old Lady Mayfeather. Lady Mayfeather was married to a mean old goat, but the lady knew everyone and everything about Devon and she was willing to talk about it. She'd loved Thea since she was a girl and the very best part was that Lord Mayfeather and Thea's father had had a falling out some years back and they rarely spoke, which meant Lady Mayfeather would hardly have a chance to tell Thea's father that she had come around asking a lot of questions about the layout of Lord Clayton's estate.

Using the map and the information she'd gleaned from Lady Mayfeather, Thea had carefully calculated the distance from the main road to the back of Lord Clayton's estate. She had ridden the pony onto the grounds but had stayed off the main path by riding through the grass and trees that bordered the northern side of the land.

Sliding off the pony, she left the horse tied up within a copse of trees. She quickly made her way to the tree line and looked out across Lord Clayton's meadows. She expelled her breath. The stables were precisely where she expected them to be. Thank heavens. By her estimation, she would only have to run less than a mile along the tree line to the building. She set off at a fast clip, hoping the black clothes she'd asked Maggie to sew for her would keep her from being seen under the moonlight.

It took Thea less than a quarter of an hour to make it to the stables. Once there, she pressed her back against the wooden side of the enormous building, breathing so heavily she could barely hear any other noises. She waited for her breathing to slow and listened for any sound in the crisp night air. Her ears were met with complete silence. The horses and their caretakers were fast asleep.

She crept along the side of the wall until she came to the first door. It was locked of course. She'd expected that. Glancing around, she found a milk carton made of wood. She picked it up and placed it beneath the window that was next to the door.

She stepped atop the wooden box and pushed at the window as quietly as possible. To her immense relief, the window moved up. It wasn't locked. She smiled to herself. That was fortunate. Using her height and pushing her legs against the side of the wall, she pulled herself up to the window and was able to perch precariously on the ledge. She stayed there for a few moments allowing her eyes to adjust to the darkness inside the stables. When she was finally convinced that it was safe, she jumped to the ground where she landed deftly on the packed earth on bent legs. Standing slowly, she glanced around. Hopefully, the noise of her entry hadn't startled any of the horses or awakened any of the stablehands.

She waited for what felt like a quarter hour before she decided it was safe to move about. The moon shone through the windows on the far side of the stables, illuminating her path enough for her to make out some of the contents of the grand building. Viscount Clayton's stables were impressive indeed. They'd clearly been designed by someone who knew a great deal about horses. The tack wall, the blacksmith's mount, the wide doors, the ropes and pitchforks and water barrels. The soaring wooden ceiling with a second floor where the stablehands slept, according to Lady Mayfeather.

The stables at Blackstone Hall were quite fine, but these, these were stunning. Fresh, fragrant bales of hay lined the walls and hung from the rafters. The stalls were the largest she'd ever seen. Each horse was housed individually in one of the stalls filled with fresh hay and the place was so clean you could probably host a dinner party inside. An enormous tack wall covered an entire side of the huge building. It smelled like leather and hay and clean horses.

Whatever else might be said of Viscount Clayton, the man certainly treated his horses well. There were *people* who didn't live this splendidly.

Thea took a few tentative steps toward the center of the building. Her heart pounded at the thought of being so near her dear Alabaster. He was here somewhere. Where was he? She made her way from stall to stall to find him.

The first stall she came to housed a sorrel mare. A gorgeous girl with markings on her nose and long, soft ears that twitched in the cool night air. The second stall held a thoroughbred. He was dark brown and clearly made for racing. The third housed one of the most gorgeous gray stallions Thea had ever seen. The next three stalls were filled with three more grays, each one as beautiful as the first. They were matching and must have cost Lord Clayton at least as much as he'd paid for Alabaster. The man certainly had money. There was no question about it.

Thea made her way past the grays. So far, all of the horses housed here were very fine indeed and all were standing, asleep, their gorgeous manes trailing along their muscled necks.

Thea was beginning to worry that Alabaster was housed elsewhere when she came to the largest stall at the far end of the row. She could see the shadow of the large black horse. She'd named him Alabaster to be ironic. She smiled at the memory. He was standing up. The moon outlined his graceful form.

It was him. Alabaster. She'd know him anywhere, even in the darkness. She quickened her pace. As she approached the stall, the horse snorted. Did he smell her? Did he know she was near? She swallowed hard. Tears stinging her eyes. At long last. Here was her horse. Her boy. He may have been barely more than a foal when she'd last seen him, but she'd know him anywhere and he appeared to remember her.

She approached the stall door with a mixture of excitement and caution. She didn't want to frighten him or excite him enough to make a louder noise. She stopped in front of the door. Heart thundering in her chest, she extended her hand, a smile on her face as the horse stepped forward to nuzzle her palm.

"There you are, my boy," she whispered as tears fell down her cheeks. "Oh, how I've missed you."

He remembered her. She could tell. She smoothed her hand over his velvety nose and muzzle. She pulled an apple from her pocket. One she'd brought specifically for this purpose. When he was younger, he'd loved the apples she'd sneaked to him.

She stood there in silence, marveling at how big he was. How magnificent. "You were in Portugal, weren't you?" she whispered finally. "I'm certain you did the King proud." She rubbed the horse's nose again.

The horse snorted again and stamped his hoof. "Don't

worry, Alabaster," she whispered. "I've made a bungle of this, but I'm going to bring you home. I promise."

Thea thought for a moment about how she'd got here, sneaking into her neighbor's stables at night. She *had* bungled everything. It had been a mistake making an enemy of Lord Clayton. As a result, he'd refused to allow her to see her horse. And he had that power. Of course she wasn't about to allow it to stop her, but she realized now that she'd made a cake of herself in front of the viscount. No doubt she'd seemed like a selfish child. No doubt she was.

One of the other horses whinnied and Thea's heart caught in her throat. She slipped into the shadows on the far side of Alabaster's stall and pressed herself against the wood planks, heart hammering in her throat. A few tense moments passed before footsteps clomped on the stairs coming down from the second floor. Thea swallowed hard. She had to get out of here.

Did she have time to run for the door before whoever was coming made it to the ground floor? From the sound of the steps, the staircase was somewhere in the middle of the stables.

She had little time to think. She decided to run for it.

Doing her best to remain in the shadows, she launched herself toward the enormous barn doors. They were locked and there was little chance she could open one herself, given their size. She had to make it back through the window she'd entered.

A large door in the middle of the nearest wall opened just as she shimmied through the window.

"Hey, there. You, stop!" came a male voice as she pushed herself through the window and landed on the cold, wet grass outside. She wasn't about to stop. Instead, she jumped up and ran toward the closest corner of the building.

Whoever was behind her was attempting to pull himself

through the window too. He must not have had the keys to the door at hand. He was still yelling at her to stop. Based on his voice, it sounded like an older man. The stablemaster, perhaps. As she turned the corner to the other side of the stables, the moon illuminated her path back toward the tree line. She had no other choice but to run. Not stopping to think, she sprinted across the field. Her feet flew beneath her kicking up clumps of grass as she went.

A commotion back at the stables met her ears as the man who'd seen her was obviously calling for assistance and other stablehands were waking up and joining him, but she didn't dare look back. Instead, she kept her eyes focused on the tree line and ran as fast as her legs would carry her. She'd always been fast. Thank heavens. Turned out chasing after her older brother all those years had been good for something.

She sprinted directly into the tree line and made her way through the copse of trees. Not until she was safe within its depths and standing at the side of her pony, did she dare to look back. Lanterns were ablaze in the stables and there were already stablehands spreading out across the meadow to search for her, but to Thea's profound relief, they were all headed in the direction of the house and the lane that led up to it. They were all moving south. She was in a copse of trees due north. Thank heavens. If she left the way she'd come and stayed in the tree line, they wouldn't see her. She hoped.

She quickly hoisted herself atop the pony and set off at a brisk pace that only increased as she left the grounds of Lord Clayton's estate. She didn't breathe easily until she was back at her house, and safely tucked inside her own bed.

As she turned over on her mattress and adjusted the pillow beneath her head, she smiled to herself. She'd got to see Alabaster. Her beloved boy. And he'd remembered her. She'd told Maggie the truth. She had no intention of stealing the horse. Stealing was beneath her. But she couldn't stand to know that Alabaster was there. So close. Without visiting him. Something about Viscount Clayton's refusal to even allow her to see the animal had made her even more stubborn than usual.

She'd nearly been caught, but it had been worth it. And despite the danger, she would go back and see her horse again. Perhaps just one last time…before the first snow fell.

CHAPTER NINE

"I'm sorry to bother you, my lord. But the horse thief returned tonight," said Humbolt, his form a silhouette inside Ewan's bedchamber door.

Ewan pushed himself up against the pillows and rubbed his tired eyes. "What bloody time is it, Humbolt?" he demanded.

"It's nearly two in the morning, my lord," Humbolt replied.

Ewan cursed under his breath. This was the second night in a row he'd been awoken from a sound sleep to the news that a thief had been chased out of his stables.

"Did he manage to steal anything tonight?" Ewan asked.

"No. Mr. Hereford chased him off again."

Ewan arched a brow. "He's not much of a horse thief, is he, Humbolt?"

Humbolt shook his head. "He was near the Arabian's stall again, my lord."

"Of course he was." Ewan shook his head. He had a strong suspicion that the person in his stables the last two nights had been none other than Lady Theodora Ballard. Even though the person who'd been seen was dressed as a lad, Ewan wouldn't put it past the chit to wear such clothing. It was either her or someone she'd sent to try to steal the horse. But something about the entire affair didn't feel right to Ewan. It didn't make sense that neither night had an attempt been made to actually *steal* the horse. The stall door hadn't been opened and the barn door hadn't even been opened. A thief, however skillful, couldn't exactly push a horse through a window. Not to mention, if the Arabian were to be stolen, the first place Ewan would look would be Lady Theodora's father's stables. If she was the thief, she had to realize it would be madness to try to take the horse from him.

But what other reason did she have for sneaking into his stables at night? Had she sent one of her father's stablehands to spy on the horse for some reason? She couldn't possibly be sneaking in merely to *visit* the animal, could she? How bloody stubborn was this young lady? Or how bloody mad?

Ewan had received a very similar report the night before. Whoever had been in the stables had managed to escape before either Mr. Hereford or the stablehands could detain him. Ewan's orders had been to be prepared if it happened again and to detain the culprit if so. Apparently, whoever it was, was a bit too surefooted for his sleepy stablehands.

"I intend to call the constable this time, my lord," Humbolt continued, "but I thought you should be aware, first."

Ewan narrowed his eyes and rubbed them, wiping the sleep from his mind. "Did anyone notice anything new tonight, Humbolt?"

"No, my lord. At least Mr. Hereford didn't mention anything."

"You said they believe it's a boy, Humbolt?" Ewan continued.

"Yes, my lord. According to the stablehands, he can't be more than twelve or thirteen years old."

Ewan rubbed his jaw and sighed loud and long. "Don't call the constable yet, Mr. Humbolt."

"My lord?" Humbolt's eyes widened in surprise. "Would you like me to have the stablemaster put someone up all night to watch the Arabian?"

"No, thank you, Humbolt," Ewan replied with another grim sigh. "I intend to catch this particular thief myself."

# CHAPTER TEN

E wan sat in the stables atop a bale of hay. The bale was pushed against the wall directly to the right of the thief's preferred window. The culprit had entered this way both times before, and Ewan hoped the chap would attempt it a third time. This was Ewan's fifth night of waiting, however, and he was both tired and impatient. After the first two nights when he'd been seen, the thief had yet to return.

Either he'd been scared off by being nearly caught twice, or he was merely waiting for the moon to be fuller. Ewan suspected that latter, which is why he had high hopes that tonight would be the night for the so-called thief's return. The moon was almost full.

Ewan had nearly drifted off. His eyes had shut just as he heard a distinctive thump against the outside wall.

He immediately sat up straight. His body tensed, ready to catch whoever this was and put an end to this nonsense once and for all.

Ewan bided his time. By all accounts the thief was slender and young. If indeed it was a lad, Ewan expected he'd be able to easily overtake the child…and if it was Lady Theodora, well, he'd easily overtake her too.

He remained crouched, alert but entirely calm, as he watched the window creak open, and the shoulders and torso of the intruder emerge. The culprit was wearing a dark cap and a black shirt with an equally dark neckcloth. No wonder the stablehands hadn't been able to see him in the meadow. As the form emerged through the window, Ewan also saw dark breeches and dark boots. He couldn't make out a face, however.

Ewan waited until the intruder was perched atop the windowsill and poised to jump to the ground inside of the stables. "Evening," he drawled, ready to pounce if the intruder tried to escape back through the window.

Instead, his voice startled the thief. The lad wobbled on the sill and fell, hitting the ground with a loud thump. The distinctive sound of a bone cracking made Ewan wince.

A half groan, half whimper came from the slight form lying on the ground. Ewan could tell the thief was doing his best not to cry out, but Ewan was certain whoever this intruder was had just broken a leg.

Ewan cursed under his breath and lit the lantern he'd hidden behind a nearby blanket. The area lit up. "You're hurt, aren't you?" he asked. He knelt down and reached for the culprit's leg to take a look.

"Don't touch me," came a slight, but extremely certain voice.

Ewan pulled his hand away. Based on the voice alone, he still wasn't certain if the intruder was a lad or Lady Theodora. "Who are you?" he asked. "And what are you doing here?"

"That's none o' yer affair," the culprit said. If it was Lady Theodora, she was obviously doing her best to disguise her speech.

"On the contrary," Ewan replied, "it's entirely my affair. You see, I own this entire estate and if you don't want me to call the constable, I'll thank you to tell me why you've been breaking into my stables."

The thief tried to jump up, presumably to run, but quickly fell to the ground again with an agonized, distinctly ladylike whimper. "Call the constable, then," the small form replied defiantly.

Ewan sat back on his heels and regarded her for a moment. Apparently, she wasn't frightened of the constable. Or if she was, she was certainly doing a fine job of maintaining her bravado. Pain was etched on the small mouth, but the culprit's cap was pulled down so low and her chin was tucked down so tightly that Ewan couldn't be entirely certain it was Lady Theodora.

But there was one way to find out.

"Very well, what if I call the doctor instead? To look at that leg," Ewan said next.

"No!" she shouted. The voice was distinctly ladylike again. He knew if it was Lady Theodora, she'd be much more worried about a doctor than the constable. The doctor might ask her to take off her breeches.

"Who are you?" he asked, narrowing his eyes on her.

She clenched her jaw and remained silent.

"Very well, you leave me no choice," Ewan said. "I'm carrying you to the house and summoning the doctor."

"What? No!" She tried to stand again and promptly fell back to the ground.

"You don't have a knife on you, do you?" he asked, certain she didn't, but cautious just the same.

"No," she nearly shouted.

"You'll forgive me if I don't quite take your word for it?" he asked as he began patting down her sides.

She squealed before nearly shouting, "Unhand me, you rogue."

Oh, yes. This was definitely Lady Theodora.

Certain of his prey, Ewan broke off his search of her pockets. "Very well, let's go." He brooked no argument. Instead, he left the lantern sitting on the dirt floor and scooped her up into his arms, doing his best not to hurt her leg, which he cradled. Despite his best efforts, she winced and whimpered, but he could tell she was trying to be brave. Grown men with broken legs would have carried on more than she was doing at the moment. It was somewhat surprising.

The moment he had her in his arms, Ewan was even more certain it was Lady Theodora herself and no young lad. First, she smelled like a woman, a hint of perfume hit his nostrils. No boy smelled anything close to that good. Second, the softness of her body gave her away along with the fact that when he pressed her to him—which, of course he did on purpose—he felt the distinctive outline of a breast through her shirt.

He cursed under his breath again. What had this chit been thinking? A broken leg was the least of her worries. Mr. Hereford might well have shot her.

Ewan stalked toward the house with her in his arms. He was silent and so was she other than the occasional futile attempt to squirm out of his arms. She was obviously not happy with his decision to take her to the house, but what alternative had she left him? And what did she possibly think she would do if she made it out of his arms? She couldn't even limp away if her leg was broken as badly as he suspected.

She was brave. He would give her that. Her jaw was tightly clenched against the ungodly amount of pain she had to be in, and her arms were locked tightly around his neck, another indication that she was a woman. No lad would be gripping him for dear life. Every once in a while, the moon hit her face in an angle where Ewan could see the sweat beaded on her brow. She might be pretending otherwise, but she was frightened.

Ewan had to handle this carefully. He knew it was her, but it could possibly cause a scandal if the servants found out who the intruder was. Loose lips in the ranks of servants certainly weren't unheard of. As he stalked toward the house, he made the decision that he would only summon a trusted few. Otherwise, he would keep the entire affair quiet until the doctor arrived and treated her leg. That was the right thing to do. Then he would send her discreetly back to her father's estate, where she would hopefully stay and stop plaguing him and his horses.

Ewan carried her into a side door of the house, through several corridors and into his study. They'd have privacy here. He set her on a large leather sofa that sat in front of a wall of windows before summoning Humbolt. Humbolt was the soul of discretion. He would ensure only a few trusted servants were aware of this incident.

When Humbolt arrived at the door to the study minutes later, Ewan saw the butler glance at the intruder before Ewan motioned for him to speak to him in the corridor. He closed the door behind him.

Humbolt's eyes were wide. "You caught the horse thief, my lord?"

"Yes, and I've reason to suspect he's broken his leg. Please send a footman to fetch Dr. Blanchard from the village. Choose a footman who will not gossip about this. Ask him to tell the doctor to come immediately."

"Of course, my lord." Humbolt bowed and disappeared into the corridor to carry out his orders.

Ewan took a deep breath and re-entered the study. Lady

Theodora was sitting up, her arms braced behind her on the sofa, wincing and staring at her broken right leg as if she were angry at it for betraying her.

Ewan grabbed a pillow from the far end of the sofa and carefully propped it under her sore leg. She winced and let out a barely audible whimper.

"I broke my leg once when I was a boy," Ewan offered. "Godawful pain. You're being quite brave."

His comment was met with stony silence.

"The doctor is on the way," Ewan offered next. But before she could deliver a pert reply, he said, "Would you care for a drink?" He moved over to the sideboard and poured some brandy into a glass.

"No," she shot back.

Ewan cocked his head to the side. "You may want to reconsider. You're sure to be in even more pain when the shock wears off. A drink might well help."

She must have seen the reason in that because she quickly replied. "Fine. I'll take it. Thank ye."

Ewan poured another glass for her and walked over and handed it to her. She took it silently, lifted the glass to her lips, and took a sip. She winced again. "This tastes like poison."

He fought his chuckle. He had to wonder if she'd ever had brandy before. Probably not. "I assure you, it's not poison. On the contrary, a duke gave me this brandy. It's quite rare."

"Rare and tasty are two different things," she mumbled under her breath, making Ewan smile again. How long would she keep up the charade that she was a boy? He wanted to find out.

"Are you going to tell me why you've been trying to steal my horse?" he ventured.

"I was not stealing!" she insisted before taking another

larger swig of brandy. She winced again, wrinkled up her nose and shook her head.

"Then why are you sneaking into my stables at night?" Ewan continued.

His question was met with defiant silence.

Ewan watched her carefully as he swirled the amber liquid in his glass. He'd taken a seat across from her in a large dark blue upholstered chair that sat at right angles from the sofa.

She squirmed under his regard and clenched her jaw. He could only imagine the pain she was in. He regretted that he'd scared her enough to cause her to injure herself, but it was frankly one of the kindest things that could have happened to her. Far better than being shot by his stablemaster. And perhaps her leg being broken would put an end to her midnight escapades.

"What is your name?" he ventured.

She swallowed and lowered her chin. But she didn't say a word. He could barely see the shadow of her face. The dark cap was still pulled so far down over her eyes that he couldn't see her features. He took in the rest of her clothing in the light. In addition to her dark breeches, her dark shirt was wrinkled, but both items of clothing looked new and all of it was far too clean to be on the back of an underaged male thief.

Ewan took another sip of brandy. "If you won't tell me your name, will you tell the doctor when he arrives? I have to send you back home somewhere."

She struggled against the sofa and pushed herself up on her hands as if to stand. "I don't need a surgeon. I intend ta leave." She made it all the way up to a standing position, bracing herself on her good leg, and hopping a bit, but the moment she attempted even one step onto her right leg, she collapsed.

Ewan lunged from his seat and caught her before she hit the floor. He carefully laid her back onto the sofa and repositioned her hurt leg with the pillow again. "I hope you'll see the reason in not attempting that again. You may as well stay and get your leg examined by the doctor," he said, keeping up the ruse. "Besides, I fear you have little choice."

"I will not stay here," she said, attempting to stand yet again.

That was it. Ewan needed to put an end to this little charade before she hurt herself even worse. The chit was more stubborn that anyone he'd ever met, and given the men he'd faced in Parliament over the years, that was saying something. "I think you have a much more pressing concern," Ewan told her.

She lifted her chin and for the first time he saw her bright gray eyes flash in the candlelight. "Wot's that?"

"How in the world you intend to convince a doctor that you're a lad, Lady Theodora." And with that, Ewan reached down and plucked the cap off her head. Dark brown hair tumbled over her shoulders.

## CHAPTER ELEVEN

How in the devil had he known it was her? Thea's skin flashed hot and cold. The room spun. She clutched the only thing she had in her hands, which was the glass of brandy Lord Clayton had given her. She lifted it to her lips and downed the entire contents in one gulp, sputtering and choking as the liquid burned its way down her throat.

Viscount Clayton's laughter filled the air. "Now that was the first intelligent thing you've done all evening," he said as he reached out and took the empty glass from her.

"What do you want from me?" Thea asked, as she tried to put her breathing back to rights. She abandoned the pretense of changing her voice to sound like a lad.

Lord Clayton cocked his head to the side and regarded her while taking a sip from his still full brandy glass. "You've got it wrong. The question is, what do *you* want from *me*? I'm not the one who's been trying to steal *your* horse."

"No," she grumbled, "you already stole him."

Lord Clayton's eyes widened. "I beg your pardon. I

purchased that horse fairly at auction and we both know it. I'm sorry that you were disappointed, but—"

She plunked her hands on her hips. "Are you sorry that you caused me to break my leg?"

His brows shot up. "If you weren't trying to steal my horse, your leg wouldn't be broken."

"I was not trying to steal anything," she insisted.

Lord Clayton cocked his head to the side. "What were you doing in the stables then? Just visiting?"

"Yes, actually."

That stopped him. For the first time since he'd been in her presence, he was at a loss for words. "You cannot be serious," he finally managed.

"You don't understand," she ground out. "Alabaster is my horse. I owned him when he was a foal. My father sold him. I—"

"Sometimes men have to do things for certain reasons that—"

Thea held up a hand. "Spare me, please. You don't know anything about why my father sold the horse." That was it. She wasn't about to try to explain anything further to Lord Clayton. He didn't care about her past. He didn't care about the fact that her father had sold both horses without even asking Thea or her mother. Lord Clayton certainly didn't care that she loved the horse. She'd already tried to tell him as much.

"You're right," Lord Clayton allowed. "I don't know."

Thea refused to be mollified by him. "As far as I'm concerned, you left me no other choice. You refused to sell him to me, Lord Clayton. You even refused to let me see him. I had to do something."

Clayton rubbed his chin and contemplated her for a moment. "May I ask you something about the horse, Lady Theodora?"

She tossed an impatient hand in the air. "Very well."

"Are you the one who named him Alabaster?"

"I did," she said, staring briefly unseeing at the carpet, remembering the day she'd first seen the perfect baby horse. He'd been such a fine foal.

"Why did you name him that?" Clayton asked. "The horse is dark as night."

The side of her mouth quirked up. "Precisely why it's the perfect name. Or does irony confuse you, my lord?" She blinked her lashes at him.

He shook his head and chuckled. "Has anyone ever told you, you have the tongue of a wasp?"

"Has anyone ever told you, you have the manners of a boar?"

"No. I suppose we're even." He shook his head again.

Thea lifted her chin. "I would like to go home, my lord. I have a pony tied in the tree line. If you would please have a footman fetch him, I will be on my way."

"You cannot ride a pony home with a broken leg, and even if you could, I wouldn't allow it. It's not safe out there at night for a female alone."

"I've traveled on my own before," she shot back. How dare this man try to tell her what to do?

"This conversation is ridiculous. You're dressed as a lad, lying on my sofa with a broken leg, and you want me to hand over a pony so you can ride home and act as if none of this ever happened?"

"Yes," she replied with a nod. "That's precisely what I want."

"Then you're either inebriated or mad."

She clenched her jaw. "I'm neither."

"Let me be clear, Lady Theodora. Despite the fact that you've been nothing but a bother to me the past few weeks,

I'm not about to send you off into the night with a broken leg."

Thea's mind raced. What were her options? If she stayed, she'd surely have to admit who she was to Dr. Blanchard. What would the doctor say? How could she possibly explain her state? If word were to get out that she'd been found alone, dressed as a lad at Lord Clayton's estate, her reputation would be in tatters. Worse, her *brother's* reputation would be in tatters.

However, Clayton was maddeningly correct in that it was ludicrous to expect that she would be able to ride her pony off into the night and pretend none of this had happened. Her leg was throbbing, and she couldn't so much as take one step, let alone mount a horse. *Blast. Blast. Blast.* Why hadn't she left well enough alone after seeing Alabaster twice?

In addition, Maggie would be worried about her. It was already past time that Thea should have returned home. Her friend would be pacing the bedchamber worrying that Thea had been shot.

Furthermore, Thea could hardly ask that a footman take a note to her home for Maggie. That would wake the servants in her household and the story would eventually get back to her father.

Thea reluctantly lifted her gaze to Lord Clayton. Under the circumstances, he was being surprisingly kind. "I didn't mean to be a bother," she grumbled, feeling not only petulant but foolish for having made such a mess of her intentions and a bit guilty for telling him he had the manners of a boar.

Lord Clayton lowered his voice, contemplating the liquid in his glass. "I should have allowed you to see the horse. I didn't realize how much it meant to you."

Thea sucked in her breath slightly. In a hundred years she wouldn't have expected odious Lord Clayton to admit he'd been wrong. She hung her head. But the truth was she'd been wrong too. She took a deep breath. This would not be pleasant to say, "I'm sorry I sneaked into your stables like a thief."

The hint of a smile quirked his lips and he looked downright…oh, for heaven's sake, handsome. She quickly pushed the thought from her traitorous mind.

"Don't worry," he continued. "I intend to keep this entire debacle as quiet as possible. At the moment only my butler is aware that you're here and he thinks you're a lad. Dr. Blanchard will have to know, of course, but we can trust him to remain silent on the matter. As soon as your leg is set, I'll have my coach put to and my servants will take you back to your father's estate as discreetly as possible."

Thea nodded slowly. That was all certainly good of him. Unexpected, but appreciated. Perhaps she might actually get back home with little fanfare or at least as little as could be expected, given the circumstances.

She managed a real smile. "Thank you."

"After my most discreet footman returns from fetching the doctor," Clayton continued, "I'll have him fetch your pony. We'll tie him to the coach. He'll return home with you."

Thea breathed a sigh of relief. "I've no idea what I'll tell my father about my leg, but I'll think of something."

Ewan inclined his head toward her. "I'll leave that to you, my lady, but you may rest assured I'll tell no one about this incident as long as you promise the next time you want to see Alabaster, you send word that you're coming, in broad daylight, dressed as a *lady* and with a proper chaperone." He gave her a smile that made her feel like her insides lit up.

She squirmed in her seat, uneasy with the feeling. "I suppose you're not *entirely* odious, my lord," she allowed.

A wide smile spread across his firm lips. "Odious? Is that what you thought of me?"

"Among a variety of other things," she admitted, smiling a bit herself despite the insistent throbbing in her leg.

"I see," came his even reply.

"I'm certain you had a few choice words for me, my lord."

He arched a brow. "I am a gentleman, my lady, and I shall not repeat them."

She leaned toward him. "Oh, come now, tell me what you thought of me the first time you met me."

He eyed her carefully, clearly trying to come up with words that would not offend her. Finally, he took a deep breath. "The truth, my lady, is that I thought—and still do—that I'd never met a more stubborn person, male or female."

She laughed despite herself. "Father always says I was born stubborn. I was supposed to be born in December, but I didn't arrive until nearly February."

Lord Clayton's clap of laughter followed. "That does not surprise me. Indeed, my lady. I'm only fortunate that you were not the one betting against me at the auction that day. I've no doubt I would have come away the loser."

She sighed. "Yes, but I would have put Father in the poor house with my bid."

A slight commotion in the corridor caught Thea's ear and she pushed herself up on the sofa, heart pounding again. Dr. Blanchard was coming. How would she ever explain herself to the doctor? Her hair was streaming over her shoulders like she was a doxy, and she was wearing breeches and a neckcloth for heaven's sake.

Lord Clayton quickly stood. "Excuse me a moment." He set down his drink and strode purposely out into the corridor, shutting the door behind him. She heard him issuing orders to the footman to collect her pony and not to say a word about it to anyone. Then Lord Clayton's voice lowered as he spoke to what was presumably the doctor for a few moments. There were some male murmurs in response, in the affirmative, before the door opened and both men stepped inside.

Clayton quickly closed the door behind them.

"Dr. Blanchard is aware of your situation, Lady Theodora, and he's agreed to complete privacy and secrecy."

"You've nothing to worry about from me, my lady," Dr. Blanchard said, hurrying to her side with his satchel and sitting on the side of the sofa next to her. "I will treat your leg and be on my way and never breathe a word about this to anyone."

Thea's shoulders relaxed for the first time since she'd fallen in the stables. Her heart pounded less fiercely in her chest. Clayton had handled the entire embarrassing explanation for her. She merely nodded in return. "Thank you, Doctor. I cannot tell you how much I appreciate your assistance…and your discretion."

The doctor nodded once. "Now let's look at that leg."

AN HOUR LATER, Thea's leg was tightly wrapped in clean, white linens that one of Lord Clayton's maids had delivered to the door without being allowed into the room. A wooden splint had been added to the wrapping to stabilize the limb. The examination and the setting of the bone had been painful to be certain, but Dr. Blanchard had been as gentle as he could. Thea was certain the brandy she'd swallowed earlier had helped. She'd begun to feel quite happy and carefree.

With her permission, Dr. Blanchard had managed to cut away enough of her breeches to get a good look at her leg. The break was below the knee, thank heavens. That, at least, had been fortunate. He'd set it and wrapped it and given her a healthy dose of laudanum, which had served to make her immediately sleepy.

"That should do it," Dr. Blanchard said as he stood and wiped his brow. "Now you must be quite careful with it. And go to sleep immediately."

"Of course," Thea replied, already barely able to keep her eyes open. "Thank you, doctor. I promise to go straight to bed as soon as I get home."

Thea pushed herself to the edge of the sofa, ready to stand...perhaps with help. She needed to get home as quickly as possible. "I shan't be a burden to you much longer, Lord Clayton," she said, addressing that remark to the viscount who had just re-entered the room after Dr. Blanchard had informed him it was all right to do so.

"If you'll kindly call your coach to take me home," Thea said to Lord Clayton.

Lord Clayton immediately turned toward the door as if he intended to do exactly that when the doctor's confused voice stopped him. "Home? My lady, you cannot go home."

Clayton stopped and swung around to face the doctor, his brows snapping together over his eyes, a thunderous look on his face.

Thea's eyes widened and she gulped. "What do you mean?" Surely, she'd misheard the doctor.

The doctor shook his head. "That is an extremely nasty break. It's not clear through the bone, but it's far worse than a mere fracture. Moving the leg any more than is necessary is entirely out of the question."

"What are you saying?" Thea managed to whisper, but her throat was closing, and it seemed as if the room was beginning to spin again.

"I mean you cannot move such a great distance, my lady. And certainly not via coach. Until your leg heals sufficiently, you must stay right here."

CHAPTER TWELVE

T he sun had barely peeked over the meadow the
next morning as Ewan paced outside the
bedchamber he'd carried Lady Theodora to last
night after Dr. Blanchard's departure. In addition to James,
the discreet footman, Ewan had chosen his most trusted
maid, Rosalie, and his housekeeper, Mrs. Cotswold. The
three servants were responsible for seeing to Lady Theodora.
If Ewan kept the knowledge of her visit to the servants who
were already aware, including Humbolt, perhaps the story of
her being there would not get out.

Ewan rubbed the back of his neck and paced some more.
Should he visit her? Should he leave her entirely alone? They
hadn't had much of a chance to speak about the situation last
night. After Dr. Blanchard left, Lady Theodora had fallen
immediately to sleep. Ewan had made the decision to carry
her upstairs himself where he'd chosen the nicest and most
feminine guest bedchamber for her. He'd summoned Mrs.
Cotswold and Rosalie to tuck Lady Theodora in and he'd
made it clear that no one outside of himself and the servants

who were already privy, should know of Lady Theodora's presence in the house.

She wouldn't be happy when she awoke. That was for certain. The look on her face when Dr. Blanchard had informed her that she wouldn't be able to go home could only be described as somewhere between horrified and aghast.

Ewan couldn't blame her. He'd been feeling quite similar emotions. How in the world would they be able to stay under the same roof for weeks? Not only were they essentially complete strangers, the two times they had met most recently, they had been at each other's throats. And now she was expected to be his houseguest for weeks? The chit was nothing but trouble as she'd proved time and time again. Granted, now she was trouble with a broken leg, but trouble just the same.

Add to that the very real danger that if anyone discovered she was here, there could be a scandal. One that might affect his political career, let alone his future marriage. What if Lady Lydia and her father found out?

Ewan wasn't entirely blameless, however. A flash of guilt shot through him. If he hadn't frightened her in the stables and made her tumble from the windowsill, she wouldn't have broken her leg. However, he mustn't forget that *she* had been the one sneaking into *his* stables. And now he was stuck with the chit for an entire month.

First thing was first, however. Ewan had had the unfortunate task of sending a missive to Lord Blackstone in the wee hours of the morning explaining the situation the best he could. He was expecting the earl's arrival at any moment.

"Are you going to pace out there all morning or come in?" came Lady Theodora's disgruntled voice from inside the bedchamber.

Ewan stopped pacing. He had to smile. What other type

of greeting did he expect from her? Last night she'd been in pain. Today the doctor had left her some medicine to alleviate it, but she still sounded grumpy. He recalled how she'd scolded him for not understanding the irony of Alabaster's name last night. Not only was she determined, she was brash, and bordering on rude. One never knew what would come out of her mouth next. Apparently, a broken leg hadn't changed that.

Forcing his face to remain completely blank, Ewan pushed open the door with one hand and peeked inside. "How did you know I was out there?"

"Who else would be wearing a hole in the floor?" she shot back.

"Are you decent?" he ventured.

A long sigh ensued. "I'm wearing a nightrail whose owner is a mystery to me and have the blankets pulled up to my armpits. I'm as decent as possible given the circumstances."

That was good enough for Ewan. He stepped inside the large white room filled with hints of light blue. His mother had always favored this room of all the guest rooms. It was the largest and the most lavishly decorated. That's why he had chosen it for Lady Theodora.

She was sitting in the middle of the enormous bed, with a nightgown pulled to her chin and blankets atop that. He could only see her head. He smothered a laugh. She was more covered than she'd been last night for certain. Her long dark hair was down around her shoulders and Rosalie must have brushed it because it was certainly not in the disarray it had been last night after he'd pulled off her cap. She looked young and pretty, despite the slight dark smudges under her eyes. She was paler than he remembered her, no doubt due to the pain in her leg. He could almost feel sorry for her. Almost.

Ewan shook off the sympathetic thoughts. "The nightgown belongs to one of the maids. I've ensured the utmost discretion," he offered, coming to stand at the end of the bed facing her.

Lady Theodora nodded. "Is it the maid who came to check on me earlier? I'll have to thank her myself."

"Yes, her name is Rosalie."

Lady Theodora gave him a wary stare. "You...aren't the one who dressed me, are you?"

He arched a brow. "Of course not. What sort of blackguard do you take me for? I carried you up here and left your care to Rosalie and Mrs. Cotswold."

Was it his imagination or did she blush? He hadn't thought she was capable of blushing.

"Thank you for that, then," Lady Theodora replied, pulling up the covers even higher, as if that were possible.

"It's highly inappropriate for me to be in your bedchamber, of course," Ewan continued, "but I suppose we've thrown convention aside long ago. How are you feeling this morning?"

Lady Theodora leaned her head back against the large pile of pillows before saying, "Every bone in my body aches if you must know."

"I'm sorry to hear that," he said, smothering another smile. "You took quite a fall last night." He refrained from saying it served her right for causing so much blasted trouble.

She emitted another long sigh. "I was an idiot. I've made a complete mess of things." She uttered the words so simply and honestly.

Ewan was taken aback by her willingness to be so truthful. "I'm pleased to hear you taking responsibility for your part in this little tragedy. Perhaps you're not *entirely* too stubborn, my lady," he said, echoing her sentiment about him being odious from the night before.

"Oh, I am. Trust me," she said, lifting a hand and waving it in the air before allowing it to drop atop the blankets again.

He chuckled at that before saying, "I took the liberty of writing to your father and—"

"You what?" She shot upright and her eyes flew open wide.

Ewan stepped back and scratched behind his ear, wincing. He was about to anger her. He could feel it. "I wrote to your father. To let him know you're here. According to James, my footman who delivered the message, your father is coming here to visit you this morning."

Lady Theodora pressed both hands to her cheeks. "Why in heaven's name did you involve my father?"

Ewan cocked his head to the side and regarded her. "Would you rather I tell no one and allow your family to think you'd been abducted or run off?" he asked calmly, rocking back and forth on his heels.

Lady Theodora emitted a disgruntled huffing noise. "I intended to write Maggie a note to let her know I was safe."

"Maggie?" he asked.

"My maid."

Ewan cleared his throat. "While that might have made you feel as if you'd done enough, but I'm afraid as a gentleman, I could not allow you to stay here without your father knowing the details of what has occurred. You must see the reason in that."

Lady Theodora wrinkled up her nose as she contemplated his words. The look on her face indicated that she clearly did *not* see the reason in it. She was about to open her mouth to no doubt say something pert or scathing when a slight knock on the door interrupted their exchange. Ewan turned to see Humbolt standing there, clearly regretting the fact that he'd had to interrupt him.

"My apologies, my lord, but Lady Theodora's father is in the drawing room. He'd like to come see her."

"Of course," Ewan replied, quickly backing out of the room. "I'll bring him up myself."

He left the room without a backward glance at Lady Theodora. He would have been beyond embarrassed if her father had known that he'd been in her bedchamber alone with her. Hopefully Lady Theodora wouldn't reveal that particular bit about her stay to Lord Blackstone.

As Ewan made his way down the corridor to the staircase, he rubbed a hand over his face. He was tired, and now he had the unenviable task of informing the earl that his unmarried daughter would have to stay at a bachelor's home for the better part of six weeks.

## CHAPTER THIRTEEN

T hea pressed her head back against the pillows on the bed and stared at the frescoed ceiling of the guest chamber for several moments. How in the world had she got herself into this mess? Oh, she knew the answer well enough. Her stubbornness. When she found herself in a mess, the answer was always her stubbornness. Her father had always told her that being stubborn was her most unattractive trait. Even Mama had told her she was too stubborn. It was true, she always had been, even to her detriment. This was certainly one of those times.

She *should* have written Lord Clayton an apology and asked nicely to visit Alabaster. She *should* have never returned after seeing the horse successfully twice. She *should* have never dressed as a lad and sneaked through a window. She *should* have done a half a score of things differently, but that didn't change the fact that she was lying in the middle of an elegantly appointed bedchamber in Lord Clayton's house wearing someone else's nightrail, about to have to explain to her father what exactly she'd done to end up here.

For some inexplicable reason, apparently Lord Clayton actually believed she would stay here while her leg healed. That was out of the question, obviously. Oh, Lord Clayton had done what he thought was right by ensconcing her in a bedchamber and informing her father of her location. He'd done the only honorable thing he could, actually, and gone above and beyond to ensure only a few trusted servants were aware of the embarrassing situation, but Lord Clayton couldn't possibly think she could *actually* remain here, despite what the doctor said. Doctors weren't concerned with things like reputations and scandals. But she certainly was. Not even so much for herself, but for Anthony. She refused to drag her innocent brother's good name through the mud. Why, Anthony would need to court and marry his future countess one day. Having a sister tainted with scandal could greatly affect his prospects.

And if all that wasn't enough reason Thea couldn't possibly stay here, there was the practical aspect to the entire affair. She barely knew the viscount. She'd angered him. He'd angered her. They may have made a tentative peace last night, but that hardly made them friends. It would be beyond embarrassing, not to mention, exceedingly awkward, to have to stay at his home for the next several weeks, an unwanted and uninvited guest based on the fact that she'd sneaked into his stables and had the misfortune—however culpable he may have been in the act—to break her fool leg.

She expelled her breath and pushed herself up against the pillows, clenching her jaw against the pain as her broken leg jostled slightly against the mattress. She wanted more laudanum, but she hadn't dared to ask for it. She needed her wits about her when she spoke to Father. He would agree with her, of course. He had to. He'd come to fetch her. She was certain of it. Why else would he travel all the way here?

Father would see the logic in needing to remove her from the house and avert potential gossip and a scandal.

Thea glanced around the elegant bedchamber. If she'd thought Lord Clayton's stables were magnificent, his home was glorious. Her own bedchamber at home wasn't this fine. In addition to the large bed that was populated with the finest of linens, the walls were papered in white with delicate blue flowers. Near the fireplace there was a seating area complete with a settee upholstered in what appeared to be light-blue silk. A sideboard near the window had a sterling silver tea set atop it. Fresh daisies rested in a white vase on her bedside table, and elegant embroidered curtains of the same light blue had been pulled back from the floor-to-ceiling windows, letting light stream through.

She eyed the gorgeous chestnut wardrobe that sat against the far wall. Were her breeches inside? She had to smile at the thought. She had little idea what she would wear to make the trip back home. Perhaps she could remain wrapped in a pile of blankets. It didn't matter. Regardless of her clothing, they'd find a way to discreetly move her to the coach without disturbing her leg and she'd simply keep it propped on pillows all the way home. That was all there was to it.

The distinct clip of two sets of boots coming down the corridor toward her bedchamber, made Thea gulp. Would Father be angry or embarrassed? Probably both. She sucked in her breath and pulled the covers up to tuck them under her armpits as she waited for the door to open.

She didn't have long to wait. Moments later, Father walked in with a look on his face that told her immediately he was indeed both angry and embarrassed. The door closed behind him and Lord Clayton's footsteps retreated in the corridor. Thea breathed a sigh of relief. At least Lord Clayton had left them to speak alone. That was decent of him.

She lowered her head, hating herself for behaving like an errant schoolgirl. Her father's censure always seemed to make her feel this way…as if she was never good enough for him and never would be.

"Theodora," his deep voice intoned, carrying with it a healthy portion of obvious disappointment.

"Father," she replied in as even a tone as she could muster, willing herself to remain calm. Perhaps she *should* have asked for that laudanum.

"Are you quite all right?" he asked first. Ever the gentleman. He had to ask after her health before he could lecture her about her behavior.

"Yes," she replied simply. "They have taken excellent care of me here." That much was true.

Her father stepped closer to her bed. He braced his fists on his hips and regarded her down the length of his nose. His voice was clipped. "I'm pleased to hear that." His lips were drawn tight. He was clearly through with niceties. "I spent the entire ride here trying to think of a reason why I would have received a letter from our neighbor, Lord Clayton, informing me that you had broken your leg at his property *in the middle of the night*. I can only assume this has something to do with that blasted horse. What in the name of God do you think you're doing?" His nostrils flared as he scowled at her.

Thea winced and swallowed hard. "I didn't precisely intend to break my leg," she began.

"Don't give me any of your sass. Why were you here in the first place?" Father's face turned to a mask of stone.

She swallowed hard again and plucked distractedly at the bed covers as she answered. "You're right. It did have to do with the horse."

Father pinched the bridge of his nose between his eyes. "Please tell me it's not true that you were trying to steal the animal."

Thea frowned. "Did Lord Clayton tell you that?"

"He told me nothing," Father shot back. "I've yet to have a chance to speak to the man much. Instead, I was summoned from bed at an ungodly hour to news that there was an urgent message from the viscount and a footman from his estate awaiting my immediate reply."

"What did his message say?" Thea asked, somewhat mollified to learn that Lord Clayton hadn't told her father that she'd tried to steal his horse. Although his answer meant that Father had just *assumed* she'd been trying to steal the horse. Not much better, really.

Father's voice was clipped. "It said you'd broken a leg on his property and the doctor has recommended that you not be moved."

Thea expelled a sigh of relief. So, Lord Clayton hadn't told Father she'd been dressed as a lad or that she'd been caught sneaking into his stables. Good. The less he knew the better.

"I broke my leg in an unfortunate accident while trying to visit Alabaster," Thea allowed. There, that was true, in addition to being less embarrassing for her.

"I understand that," Father clipped. "But why in heaven's name were you sneaking about *in the middle of the night*? Why didn't you visit during the day, with a chaperone? Or better yet, why did you come at all? Lord Clayton won the auction fairly and you know it."

Thea lowered her head. Her father had the ability to make her feel like a recalcitrant child no matter her age. The worst part was, he wasn't entirely wrong. She'd acted like a selfish, spoiled little monster. And she had a broken leg to show for it.

"I'm sorry, Father." She continued to trace a finger around the little embroidered blue flowers on the bedspread so she wouldn't have to see her father's disapproval.

"And *I'm* sorry we didn't win the auction, Theodora, but that's hardly a reason for you to behave in this manner."

There was only one way to handle this. Be as contrite and apologetic as possible and convince him to take her home immediately. Arguing with her father would only extend her stay in this bed, in this house. "I know," she began. "And I agree with you. My behavior has been abominable. I've apologized to you and I shall apologize again to Lord Clayton. I'm quite sorry for my behavior and I promise never to sneak over here again. Now please take me home." She finished her little apology speech with a resolute nod. There. That was what the man wanted to hear, wasn't it? She'd made her atonements. She lifted her chin and met her father's gaze.

To her surprise, Father's eyebrows shot up. "Take you home?" His voice was filled with disbelief.

Thea narrowed her eyes. A sinking feeling began to spread in her middle. "Yes, we're going home now, aren't we?"

"Absolutely not. I spoke with Dr. Blanchard downstairs in the drawing room while I was waiting. He's come to check on you this morning and shall be up here after we finish speaking. He was quite clear about you not being moved until your leg heals."

Panic began to claw at Thea's insides. Panic mixed with nausea. "I know he said that, but surely we can be careful on the ride home."

Her father shook his head. "The ride home is long and bumpy. According to the doctor, we could do irreparable harm to your leg. He said you would be likely to walk with a limp if it doesn't heal correctly."

Thea gulped. A limp? That didn't sound particularly pleasant. But she was willing to take the risk if it meant escaping Viscount Clayton's house. "Well, I cannot possibly stay here. I'm not welcome." There. That was irrefutable logic.

"On the contrary, I've only spoken to Viscount Clayton briefly and intend to speak to him at greater length before I leave, but on the walk up here he mentioned that he's entirely amenable to your remaining here while you convalesce. He realizes how serious the situation is. It's quite good of him. You should be thankful."

"Amenable? Thankful?" she repeated. The panic rose in her throat making her voice high and thin. "The viscount was just being gentlemanly, Father. He doesn't want me here anymore than I want to be here." She could not believe her father was actually contemplating leaving her here. She pressed a hand against her belly. She might just cast up her accounts.

Her father shrugged. "I doubt Clayton relishes the situation, but it's extremely good of him to offer his home and his servants for your care. You're being ungrateful, Theodora."

Thea clamped her mouth shut. This couldn't possibly be happening. Was she trapped in a nightmare? Had the laudanum made her delirious? Father had to see reason. "You cannot possibly believe I can stay here for any length of time without the possibility of a scandal. If word gets out that I'm here, the entire countryside will conjecture as to how I got here. And it will take no time at all for word to spread all the way to the *ton* in London."

Father arched brow. "I agree. That is a very real possibility. And you should have thought of *that* before you sneaked here in the middle of the night." Anger and disapproval dripped from her father's tone.

"Father, please!" Thea was desperate. "Think about our family's reputation. Think about Anthony. If this becomes a scandal, it could hurt his future prospects."

Father's nostrils flared and he turned toward the door. "It could," he agreed. "And I intend to leave it to *you* to explain to your brother why you've made the choices you've made. Now, I'm leaving. I've brought Maggie with me. She packed a trunk with some of your belongings that you'll need. She'll remain with you as a chaperone and caretaker, so you won't be as much of a burden on Lord Clayton and his staff. Clayton intends to tell his servants that Maggie is newly hired by him."

"That won't work. There is certain to be gossip." Thea tried to push off the covers and move to the side of the bed to stand, but the throbbing pain in her leg was too much. She gritted her teeth in frustration. "You cannot leave me here, Father! Who will plan our Christmastide ball?" She knew such an argument was ludicrous at this point, but desperation was muddling her brain.

Her father's hand was already on the door handle. "On the contrary, Theodora. I *can* leave you here and that's exactly what I intend to do. The servants will plan the ball. You'll be home in time for it, don't worry." He opened the door and turned to face her. "In the meantime, perhaps you will act better as a guest in Lord Clayton's home than you do as a resident in mine."

He turned to leave and was about to step into the corridor when Thea asked in a near shriek, "How long must I stay here? A sennight? A fortnight?"

Father paused and turned his head to the side. "Until your leg heals."

Thea forced herself to take a deep breath. "Heals? For goodness sake, how long will that be?"

Father's monotone answer floated back to her. "At least a month, according to Dr. Blanchard."

"A month," Thea echoed, nausea roiling in her belly. "I

cannot stay here a month. Surely it will be safe enough to travel sooner than a month."

"The doctor is not convinced. Now, I intend to go speak with Viscount Clayton further about the details. I shall tell him that you will be on your best behavior, Theodora. Do *not* make me a liar."

## CHAPTER FOURTEEN

The slight knock at the door to his study made Ewan glance up from the ledgers he'd been reviewing. "Come in," he called.

The door opened and the Earl of Blackstone stepped inside. The older man had a resigned and decidedly unhappy look on his face.

Ewan pushed back his chair and stood. "Would you like a drink, Blackstone?" It may have been morning, but under the circumstances, Ewan thought a drink might well be in order.

"No, thank you, Clayton. I hope not to take much more of your time than you've already been forced to give my family over the last twenty-four hours."

"It's no trouble, my lord," Ewan replied. He felt a bit sorry for the man. Blackstone obviously had a high-spirited daughter who was prone to get into trouble. It wasn't as if the earl could keep an eye on the chit constantly.

"It *is* trouble, Clayton," Blackstone replied, "but you're a good man to help us."

"Please take a seat," Ewan offered, splaying his hand toward one of the two chairs that sat facing his desk.

Blackstone lowered himself into the seat closest to the door and sighed. "I'm afraid when my daughter gets something in her head, she cannot be dissuaded."

Ewan chuckled. "So I've come to learn about her, my lord."

Blackstone leaned back. "The horse, the Arabian. She believes it belongs to her, or should at least, because we owned him once."

Ewan nodded. "Yes, my lord. I understand."

"I'm not excusing her behavior, mind you," Blackstone continued. "I simply wanted to tell you why she's caused you so much trouble. Even still, she wants to purchase the animal." The older man shook his head.

"Yes," Ewan replied, nodding. "Did Lady Theodora tell you she offered me double the price I paid at auction?"

Blackstone's brows shot up. "What? No. We don't have *that* amount of money. And even if we did, I wouldn't spend it on one horse for heaven's sake."

"I don't blame you," Ewan replied. "Rest assured I declined her offer."

"I blame myself for her shortcomings," Blackstone continued with a sigh. "Her mother died when she was younger and, well, I've always thought she lacked a woman's guiding hand these last few years. Perhaps I should have married again and provided her with a stepmother. Instead, I've appeased Theodora as much as I could. The Arabian, however, was a step too far. I should never have agreed to send Anthony to attempt to buy him back."

Ewan eyed the man carefully. Lord Blackstone seemed a reasonable sort, but there was still one outstanding question that bothered Ewan. "May I ask why you sold the horse, my lord, if it meant so much to your daughter as a pet?"

Blackstone shrugged and contemplated his fingernails. "Harlowe offered me an amount I couldn't refuse. Apparently that horse is from an unimpeachable bloodline. My late wife had been the one to pick out his mother and breed her. Thea's mother was a fine judge of horseflesh. How was I to know my daughter would take the horse's absence so personally?"

*You might have asked her*, Ewan thought as he stared at the man. Clearly, Lord Blackstone wasn't one to worry much about the feelings of those close to him. For the second time that day, Ewan felt a bit sorry for Lady Theodora. He'd already decided that he had no intention of telling Blackstone that his daughter had sneaked into his stables on at least three occasions in the middle of the night. Blackstone's flippant attitude toward the young lady made Ewan confirm that decision. Further, Ewan had no intention of revealing to the earl that his only daughter had been dressed as a lad when she'd done it. "I see," Ewan replied simply.

Blackstone shook his head again. "Theodora is the most stubborn girl I have ever known. The most stubborn *person*."

Ewan smiled. "Don't judge her too harshly, Lord Blackstone. It's a good trait to have. I've found myself thinking that it's too bad she cannot be an army officer. I fear the French would surrender immediately if faced with Lady Theodora across a battlefield."

Lord Blackstone chuckled. "Seems you've already come to know my daughter a bit, my lord. I am sorry that she'll be an inconvenience to you. I understand Dr. Blanchard has said she shouldn't move."

"That's right. He fears the journey home might be too much for the fractured bone. It might make it a clean break."

Blackstone opened his coat and pulled out a small leather purse from an inside pocket. "I'm prepared to pay for her expenses while she's here, room and board, of course. And anything else she requires. Please send all her bills to me." The earl opened the purse and removed several large bills.

Ewan waved the money away. "That will not be necessary, my lord. I intend to treat her as an honored guest. She is my neighbor, after all."

Blackstone frowned. "She is not your burden, my lord." He sighed. "She is mine."

"Be that as it may," Ewan replied, thinking it was hardly fatherly of the earl to refer to his only daughter as a 'burden,' "I do not require funds to keep her here."

Blackstone gave Ewan a look that clearly indicated he thought the viscount was a bit mad, but he stuffed the bills back into his purse and returned the pouch to his coat pocket. "Very well. I'll leave her to you with her chaperone, Maggie, and one of our footmen, Giles. I've given Maggie instructions to send me a message via Giles should Theodora require anything from me while she is here."

"Thank you, my lord. You have my word that I will do everything in my power to ensure the news of her presence here is a closely guarded secret. However, if anyone finds out, we can always say she was here visiting the horse and broke her leg while riding."

Blackstone gave him a skeptical glance. "If that was the way scandals worked, Clayton, I would agree with you, but if word leaks that she was here in the middle of the night, I'm afraid no amount of storytelling will make it right."

"I cannot argue with you there, my lord," Ewan replied, standing and escorting the man to the door. "Regardless, rest assured that your daughter will be entirely comfortable during her stay."

Lord Blackstone opened the door and glanced back at Ewan. "Don't make her too comfortable, Clayton. She could use a bit of discomfort, that one."

CHAPTER FIFTEEN

No sooner had Dr. Blanchard left after checking on her, than the door to Thea's bedchamber opened again and Maggie rushed inside. The maid came hurrying to Thea's bed, her eyes bright with worry. "Are you quite all right, Thea?"

Without waiting for an answer, Maggie flipped the covers back to see Thea's injury. She gasped and stepped back as soon as she saw her black and blue leg. The bruises were visible above and below the white bandages. "Oh, dear. It looks awful," Maggie breathed.

"It *is* awful," Thea allowed, pulling the covers back to hide her leg. "But the leg is the least of my concerns at the moment."

"Your father informed me that we're to stay here … for *weeks*," Maggie said, surprise obvious on her features.

"Father has quite lost his mind," Thea retorted.

"Just now as he was leaving, he mentioned something about a limp," Maggie replied. "It didn't sound good at all."

Thea pounded her fist atop the mattress. "Is a limp worse than being ruined? Than Anthony being ruined? If anyone learns that I've been here, our family name will be dragged through the mud. But apparently, Father doesn't care about that."

"It does seem rather short-sighted of him," Maggie replied, wringing her hands. "Surely there are precautions that could be taken with your leg to get you home."

"My thoughts exactly," Thea replied. "But he wouldn't hear of it."

Maggie bit her lip. "Your father asked me to pretend as if I am newly hired by Lord Clayton."

"As if that won't generate gossip belowstairs," Thea replied, rolling her eyes.

"I was thinking the same thing," Maggie said.

"So, apparently, we'll be staying here for at least a month," Maggie continued, with a sigh. She walked around in a circle, taking in the details of the large room. "At least it's a beautiful bedchamber. From what I've seen, the house is well taken care of. This room is quite large and finely decorated. Lord Clayton must have quite a fortune."

"Yes, but we won't be remaining here that long if I can help it," Thea replied, arching a brow.

Maggie whirled around to face her. "Oh, no. Please don't tell me you're thinking of trying to escape with a broken leg."

A triumphant smile spread over Thea's lips. "Of course not. That would be dangerous and difficult."

"As if that's stopped you before," Maggie replied, crossing her arms over her chest.

Thea pursed her lips and lifted her nose in the air. "Be that as it may, I have an entirely different plan this time."

Maggie groaned and let her chin drop to her chest. "Do I even want to know what it is?"

"I don't see why not. It's perfectly reasonable and level-headed," Thea declared with a decisive nod.

"Very well," Maggie said with a sigh, lifting her chin to face Thea again. "What is it?"

Thea folded her hands together primly and set them atop the blankets. "I intend to write to Anthony and ask him to come fetch us."

# CHAPTER SIXTEEN

E wan spent an inordinate amount of time wondering whether he should ask Lady Theodora if she would like to have dinner with him either in the dining room or in her room. Her presence was a secret from all but a few in the household, of course, so he didn't see what harm it would cause if they ate dinner alone in her bedchamber. And there would be servants present as chaperones.

He eventually decided that it would be rude to completely ignore her, so he sent a note to her room via James, the footman. Ewan didn't have long to wait until she replied that she would be delighted to have dinner with him. *Delighted* seemed a bit of a stretch. Perhaps the laudanum had made her nicer. Or madder?

At exactly eight o'clock that evening, Ewan knocked on Lady Theodora's bedchamber door. Her maid—Maggie, he believed her name was—answered the door and stepped aside, allowing him entry.

Lady Theodora was sitting atop the bed. She was dressed in a light blue gown, her hair arranged artfully atop her head, and the covers pulled down to her feet. He could imagine she was shoeless, but she had on stockings and her feet were covered by the blankets. A tray sat on her lap and a napkin and utensils rested there. She had a bright smile on her face. "Good evening, my lord," she said, bowing her head in a greeting.

Ewan couldn't help but smile in return. "Good evening, my lady." He bowed at the waist. "I trust you're comfortable. Or as comfortable as you can be given the circumstances."

She sighed. "My leg still hurts quite a lot, if I'm being honest, but the occasional bit of laudanum Maggie gives me keeps it from being unbearable."

Ewan glanced at the maid who barely looked up from her needlework to acknowledge him. "Thank you for coming here, Maggie. And thank you for your assistance in pretending to be employed by me."

"My pleasure," Maggie replied, before returning her attention to her needlework.

The footmen had set a small table next to the bed and covered it in linens and all the accoutrements necessarily for a meal. One chair was tucked beneath the table. It might have been the strangest dinner Ewan had ever attended, but everything had been strange since he'd met Lady Theodora Ballard. Why should this be any different?

"May I?" Ewan asked, gesturing toward the chair.

"By all means," Lady Theodora replied, nodding.

Ewan pulled out the chair and seated himself, while James rushed forward to pour wine into his empty glass. Giles also stepped forward to pour wine into Lady Theodora's glass.

"I trust you've found your accommodations to your liking?" Ewan ventured as he waited for the footmen to finish their task.

"Oh, my bedchamber is absolutely lovely," Thea replied, glancing around the large space. "And while we're on the subject, I must tell you that your stables are the nicest I've ever seen."

"I take that as a great compliment, my lady. Thank you." The first course of watercress soup was served before Ewan ventured to speak again. "I'll have to see what I can do about procuring a special chair for you, my lady."

Lady Theodora glanced up at him and blinked. "A special chair? What do you mean?"

"Dr. Blanchard told me that the apothecary has a Bath wheelchair. I intend to purchase it for you."

Lady Theodora's eyes widened, and a look of sheer panic spread rapidly across her face. "Oh, no, no, no. Please don't go to any trouble for me. I've already been such a bother."

Ewan frowned. Had her father told her she was a bother to him? Frankly, Ewan wouldn't have put it past the man. "No bother at all. It will help you to do more things while you're here like sit near the window and perhaps even venture out of the room."

Lady Theodora continued to shake her head. "No, truly. Please don't go to such an expense on my account."

"If you're to stay here for at least a month, my lady, we may as well make the best of it. We have no other choice it seems."

Lady Theodora ducked her head. "Yes, yes, of course. That sounds lovely."

Ewan eyed her bent head with suspicion. Why wouldn't she meet his gaze? What was she up to? He could ask her, but she would hardly be forthcoming. Instead, he decided to bring up something else he wondered about, her relationship with her father.

"I spoke with your father this morning," Ewan began, lifting a spoonful of soup to his lips.

Was it his imagination or did Lady Theodora's face turn

to stone at the mention of her father? "Yes," she replied simply, no emotion in her voice.

"He told me something I'm ashamed to admit I had forgotten," Ewan continued.

Lady Theodora paused in bringing her own soup spoon to her lips. "What's that, my lord?"

"That your mother died several years ago."

Lady Theodora's gaze dropped to her spoon and she brought it to her lips and swallowed before replying. "Yes," she replied simply.

What was this? The young woman he'd known to trade sharp jabs with him was now replying with monosyllabic words. Was it the laudanum? Or had she simply realized the error of her ways and was purposely behaving like a proper young lady? And more importantly, why did Ewan find himself missing the girl he'd traded barbs with?

"I'm sorry," he replied. "It must have been difficult for you to lose her. How old were you?"

"Eighteen." Lady Theodora set down her spoon and stared across the room as if unseeing. "It was the worst time of my life."

"No doubt," Ewan replied quietly. "Was she ill for very long?"

"Yes. Months. I was at her bedside taking care of her day and night."

Ewan's brow furrowed into a knot. Until this moment, he couldn't have pictured Lady Theodora working as a nurse at someone's beck and call around the clock. But watching her face, he knew without a doubt that she was telling the truth.

"How soon after her death did your father sell the horses?" Ewan ventured.

Anger flashed through Lady Theodora's eyes and for a moment, Ewan wondered whether he should have brought up the obviously sensitive subject.

"They were sold even before my mother took her last breath," Lady Theodora said, her voice thin but with an unmistakable trace of anger. "I didn't know because I hadn't been out to the stables in weeks. I knew it was close to my mother's time and I refused to leave her alone. My mother's horse meant the world to her, as did Alabaster to me."

Ewan expelled his breath. Guilt tinged his voice. "So that's why Alabaster is so important to you."

Lady Theodora nodded. Her eyes were bright with a sheen of tears. "I lost the two souls that were the closest to me in this world. My mother, and my horse." She took a deep, steady breath. "The horse was the only one I had any chance of regaining."

Ewan felt as if he'd been punched in the gut. He didn't miss Maggie look up from her needlework, tears on her cheeks. As soon as the maid noticed that he'd glanced over, however, she quickly swiped the tears away and bent her head back over her needlework.

For the first time in his dealings with Lady Theodora, Ewan felt like a complete ass. The ass she'd called him on the day they'd met. He'd never asked her reasons for wanting Alabaster so badly. He'd merely assumed she wanted the horse because he'd been hers once and she didn't like losing a treasured possession. But Alabaster wasn't just a possession to her. He was her family.

They finished their meal trading little more than small talk and niceties. Ewan left Lady Theodora's room that evening with a heavy heart. He'd pegged the young woman as selfish and self-absorbed, but the truth was she'd apparently given up months of her young life to care for her ailing mother. That was definitely not selfish. He'd misjudged Lady Theodora on that score. What else had he misjudged her about?

# CHAPTER SEVENTEEN

"Have you heard back from Lord Anthony yet, my lady?" Maggie asked Thea the next morning after she'd helped her dress.

"Not yet," Thea replied. She was sitting atop the covers on the made bed, her leg propped upon pillows, busily sewing a new nightrail for Rosalie, the maid who'd been so kind to allow Thea to borrow hers the night she'd broken her leg. "Perhaps he doesn't intend to write. My hope is that he will simply appear with a coach and four and take us home. Much more efficient, don't you think?" Thea finished with a laugh.

Maggie shook her head. "Do you truly think he will?"

Thea nodded firmly. "Anthony won't leave me here to rot. I'm certain of it." She returned to her needlework and her thoughts about the dinner last night with Lord Clayton. It had been kind of him to have dinner with her. He easily could have left her shut in the room and just sent up a plate. Instead, he'd treated her as a real guest. Not only that, he had somehow managed to ask her about one of the most painful subjects in her life and got her to answer. Thea never talked about losing her mother, never. But somehow, with just a few short questions, Lord Clayton had convinced her to share her deepest feelings with him. How in the world he had managed that, she didn't know. But she mustn't spend too much time worrying about it. She had to find a way to get back home. If Anthony didn't come soon, she would write him again.

Thea had just slipped the needle back into the soft white linen of the nightrail when a loud knock on her bedchamber door made her sit up straight. Maggie met her gaze from her seat near the window. They exchanged a puzzled look before the maid stood, set her embroidery in her chair, and made her way to the door.

The minute the door opened, Lord Clayton came barreling through pushing a wheelchair in front of him.

"Good morning, my lady," he said with a bright smile, addressing Thea.

"Good morning, my lord," Thea replied with a similar smile. "What is that?" She gestured toward the chair.

Clayton pushed the wheelchair to the side of her bed. "This is your new wheelchair. I sent James and Giles to town for it early this morning."

Thea couldn't help her delighted smile. The chair was shaped like a triangular box with two large wheels at the back and one wheel in front. There was a smaller square box above the front wheel that had a handle atop it and two handles on both sides. Thea stared at it in awe. "You did this for me?" She pointed at herself.

"Of course. It will ensure that your leg is stabilized, and it will make it so that you can get about the house with less trouble. You don't want to spend your entire stay hidden away in this room, do you?"

Thea blinked at him. She'd honestly believed she *would* have to spend her entire stay hidden away in this room, not just because of the trouble of moving about with a broken leg, but also because they were trying to keep her presence here a secret. Not to mention the fact that she expected Anthony to arrive at any moment and take her home. A bit of guilt tugged at her conscience. Lord Clayton must have spent quite a lot of coin on this chair, and she was going to leave here the first chance she got. "I hadn't expected you to procure one so quickly."

"After we spoke about it last night, I decided to send for it right away," Lord Clayton replied.

Thea's eyes met his. "That was quite kind of you, my lord," she said softly. Their gazes held for a long moment before Thea forced herself to look away and shook her head. "Oh, Mag, do come help me to sit in it." If the man had gone to the trouble to get her a wheelchair, it would be extremely rude of her not to use it and be thankful for it. Even if only for a day or two…

"No need," Lord Clayton said, waving away the maid as he pushed the chair up to the end of Thea's bed and stepped around it. "I'll help you."

Thea barely had a moment to register his words before she was unceremoniously scooped up into his arms, broken leg, splint, and all.

She clutched at his shoulder and wrapped her arms around his neck to keep from tipping back, all the while intensely aware of the spicy scent of his cologne and the feel of his muscled arms moving beneath her. Her gaze inadvertently moved to his mouth of all inconvenient places to stop. His firmly molded lips were only scant inches from hers. Thea sucked in her breath. What would it be like to…kiss him? She gulped and glanced away.

Then, just as quickly as he'd lifted her, Lord Clayton set

her down in the chair as easily as you please. He even managed to maneuver her broken leg into a wooden contraption on the side of the chair that kept her leg lifted and stabilized.

"I've never seen a wheelchair with such an apparatus," Thea said, more to distract herself from the memory of his muscles and mouth than anything else.

"I made that part myself," Lord Clayton replied, looking a bit sheepish.

"You what?" Thea blinked at him some more. Surely, she'd misheard him.

Lord Clayton rubbed the back of his neck and squinted. "Last night, before I went to bed, I was thinking about how we could keep your leg stabilized inside the chair. I couldn't sleep so I drew a sketch and then went out to the barn to create it."

"Are you quite serious?" Thea exchanged a brief surprised glance with Maggie who lifted her eyebrows and stepped back toward her chair. "How in the world were you able to make it so quickly?"

"I… I like to… experiment with things." Lord Clayton trailed off before scrubbing a hand across his forehead. "I do hope you don't find it too forward of me."

Thea smiled at him and shook her head. "No more forward than me breaking my leg in your stables, my lord." She reached out and touched his shoulder. "Thank you. I am delighted to have this chair. It's perfect."

Their gazes met again, and Thea was mesmerized by the look in his blue eyes. It was beyond generous of him to not only procure the chair for her, but to go to the trouble of making a special splint for her leg.

Not to mention the fact that he could have just sent the chair up with the footmen and asked them to help her into it, but he'd delivered it and helped her himself. Lord Clayton's gaze rested on her hand, which was still touching him. She quickly snatched it away as if it had been burnt and cleared her throat. "I greatly appreciate it, my lord. I'm certain my father will reimburse you—"

"Rubbish," Lord Clayton replied, waving away her words. "This is a gift. An unusual one, granted, but a gift, nevertheless. Now, shall I help you learn to use it in the corridor?"

THEA SPENT the better part of the next hour out in the corridor learning how to use the handles on the sides of the square box to propel herself in the wheelchair. It was exhausting and she wasn't entirely certain she was doing it correctly, but she made enough progress to be able to go short distances by herself. She would have to rely on the footmen and Maggie to go longer distances in the chair, but at least Thea learned how to move around a bit.

Lord Clayton took his leave about halfway through her lesson when Mr. Humbolt arrived and informed him that his solicitor was waiting in the study to go over the books with him. Thea had felt a brief pang of disappointment when Lord Clayton had been forced to leave, but she quickly continued her lesson with Maggie and Rosalie's help and soon the three young ladies were in hysterics over Thea's penchant for rolling herself into corners and getting stuck.

When they returned to the bedchamber, Thea found herself happy but thoroughly drained. "I think I need a nap," she informed Maggie the moment the bedchamber door closed.

"Would you like me to summon Lord Clayton to help you back into bed?" Maggie asked, her eyebrows waggling.

Thea slapped at her friend. "Absolutely not. I'm certain

the three of us can manage if we just put our minds to it." She gestured to Maggie and Rosalie.

With the maids' help, Thea stood from the chair and hopped back toward the bed. It was slow, uncomfortable, and somewhat painful. The entire process was much more difficult than when Lord Clayton had deftly scooped her up and sat her in the wheelchair. But she couldn't very well rely on him to move her back and forth. Not only would that be an unreasonable request, it would be beyond embarrassing. Especially given what had happened when he'd moved her earlier. The last thing she needed was to have another moment of feeling his muscles and thinking about what it would be like to kiss him. Besides, Anthony would be coming for her soon and she would be whisked back to Blackstone Hall. She had to learn how to manage a broken leg *without* Lord Clayton.

Wincing, Thea pulled herself atop the mattress. Maggie had already pulled back the covers, while Rosalie helped her to scooch against the pillows before she pulled the covers over Thea's legs.

"Thank you, Rosalie," Thea said, settling back against the pillows and expelling her breath. In addition to some rest, she needed a bit of laudanum. Her leg was throbbing again. "I appreciate your help. And your discretion." It couldn't hurt to remind the maid that her presence here was still a secret.

"Oh, don't ye worry none, me lady," Rosalie said, nodding sagely. "I'm an old hand at keeping things quiet 'round 'ere. I've got lots o' practice." She glanced over each shoulder and lowered her voice, bending closer to Thea. "Ye see, ye're not the only secret houseguest staying 'ere, me lady. There's another wot's down the far end o' the corridor, in the next wing."

Thea's eyes went wide, and her throat went dry. "*What?*" She blinked rapidly, quite unable to believe what she was hearing. Could what the maid was telling her be true? And if it was true, who in heaven's name was Lord Clayton's *other* secret houseguest?

"It's true, me lady," Rosalie said, as if she'd read Thea's thoughts. "Only, even I'm not privy to that guest. I've no idea who's in that room."

# CHAPTER EIGHTEEN

E wan decided to ask James and Giles to bring Lady Theodora and her wheelchair into the dining room that evening. The two footmen waited until no other servants were in the foyer before carrying her down and pushing her into the large room. Ewan was standing near the windows with his hands in his pockets when they entered. He turned immediately to greet her and immediately sucked in his breath.

Lady Theodora was wearing a pretty gown of lavender and her hair was swept up. A string of pearls graced her neck and earbobs hung from her ears. She was breathtaking.

"You look wonderful," Ewan told her, thinking he'd never had a more lovely dinner partner. He moved away from the window to meet her near the table.

"So do you, my lord," Lady Theodora replied, her gaze taking him in from top to toe.

Ewan glanced down. He had spent some time on his appearance this evening, ensuring that his valet put him in his finest evening attire, including a black coat and breeches, white shirtfront and cravat and a sapphire blue waistcoat.

He'd even bothered to slick back his hair with a bit of pomade.

Ewan bowed to Lady Theodora, "Thank you, my lady. I'm pleased that you agreed to have dinner with me again this evening."

"No, it is I who must thank you," Lady Theodora replied. "It's lovely to come sit in a dining room again and to feel as if everything is somewhat normal."

Ewan chuckled. "I can understand that sentiment." He gestured to the dinner table that had already been set by the servants. The two footmen had gone down to the kitchens to retrieve the first course.

"May I?" Ewan asked, gesturing to Lady Theodora's chair.

"Yes, please," she replied, giving him a smile.

Ewan pushed her chair up to the table as close as possible. He angled the seat so that her legs were to the right side of the head of the table. "I took the liberty of moving my place setting closer to yours. I hope you don't mind."

Lady Theodora glanced down at the tabletop where Ewan's plates, utensils, and wine glass were set on the left side of hers.

She gave him another bright smile. "I prefer it, actually. That way we'll be able to hear one another." She laughed as she regarded the long stretch of the dining table.

"That was my thinking as well. Why stand on formality?" Ewan replied, grinning. "We're already in an odd arrangement."

"Indeed," Lady Theodora replied.

The footmen entered the room with the first course of artichoke soup and began to serve it and pour the wine.

Lady Theodora cleared her throat. "Did you…finish your business with your solicitor, my lord?"

Ewan grabbed up his spoon. "Yes, though I can't say it was more enjoyable than helping you with your wheelchair lessons. How about you? What did you do this afternoon? After your lesson, that is."

Lady Theodora laughed again, and Ewan realized it was a pleasant sound. Much more preferable than her waspishness. "I rested a bit, and I woke with sore arms." She winced and pressed her shoulders. "And then I finished sewing the nightrail."

Ewan frowned. "Nightrail?"

Lady Theodora nodded and took a sip from her wine glass. "Yes, I sewed a nightrail for Rosalie."

The frown remained on Ewan's face. "Rosalie? The maid."

"That's right. She was so kind as to allow me to wear one of hers the night I came to stay here, I thought it only right to repay her with a new garment. Maggie brought some fabric from home. It is the loveliest white sarcenet."

Ewan stared hard at Lady Theodora for several seconds before he finally realized he was gaping at her. "That was... good of you," he finally managed.

Lady Theodora shrugged. "No better than what she did for me. And speaking of nice gestures, thank you again for the wheelchair, my lord. It was entirely unexpected and unnecessary but appreciated just the same."

Ewan shook his head and took another sip of wine. "Don't mention it again, please. It's the least I could do for you."

Lady Theodora took another spoonful of soup. "Yes, you mentioned having the chair would help me to move around the house and property. Am I allowed to go *anywhere* on the property then, my lord?" She eyed him expectantly.

Ewan furrowed his brow. "Yes. I don't see why not. We can arrange for the servants who don't know you're here to be out of a certain area when you visit if that's what you mean."

She leaned forward farther, still eyeing him carefully. "Anywhere? There's *nowhere* that is off limits?"

Ewan frowned. "If you mean the stables, I can definitely help you get out there. I may need to inform a couple of the stablehands that you'll be there. That would expose more people to your secret. But if you're fine with that—"

"Oh, I would *love* to go to the stables," Lady Theodora replied. "But I actually meant to ask about the house itself. Am I allowed to go *anywhere* in the house?" She continued to eye him as if she was expecting him to suddenly come up with an area that was off limits.

Ewan narrowed his eyes on her. "I don't understand. Is there somewhere in the house you particularly wish to go, my lady?"

She quickly reverted her attention to her meal and poked her spoon idly around her soup bowl for a few moments. "Oh, no. Nowhere in particular. I just wouldn't want to go somewhere I wasn't welcome."

Ewan shook his head. "If you need help getting around, I'm happy to assist you."

"Thank you, Lord Clayton. I appreciate that."

Ewan cleared his throat. Now was the perfect time to bring up a subject he'd been meaning to. "Yes, as to that, after living under my roof, I feel as if you should call me Ewan."

Surprise registered for just a moment on Lady Theodora's face before it was replaced with a bright smile. "Very well. You may call me Thea, if you like."

"Thea?" He cocked his head to the side. "Not Theodora?"

She chuckled. "No one calls me Theodora." She drew out the long name and said it in an overly formal tone as if mocking it.

"Your father does," Ewan pointed out.

Her eyes turned hard. "No one but my father calls me Theodora," she clarified, her voice flat.

It was time to change the subject. After last night's debacle where he'd clearly made her sad by bringing up her lost mother and her former horse, Ewan was desperate to keep the discussion light this evening.

"Have you been to London much?" Ewan asked next as the footmen cleared the soup bowls and served the next course of mackerel with fennel and mint. "I don't remember seeing you at many events."

"I never go to London," Thea replied simply. "I prefer the countryside."

"Don't you miss your friends?" Ewan asked.

She chuckled. "Maggie is my best friend."

"Maggie?" He furrowed his brow. "Your maid?"

Thea nodded. "I suppose that seems unconventional of me to someone like you, but—"

He arched a brow. "Someone like me? What does that mean?"

Thea smiled and shook her head slightly. "I'm sorry, my lord…Ewan. I only meant that you seem to be quite…conventional."

His brow remained arched. "Conventional?" He wasn't certain he liked the sound of that particular word.

"Yes, you know. Father told me you're extremely interested in politics, which means I assume you like to follow rules and do things properly and, you know, follow conventions."

Ewan took another sip of wine. "Why in the world would you assume that?"

Thea waved her fork in the air. "Politics seem so proper and, well, conventional."

"Would you be interested to know I'm a scientist?"

Thea bit her lip. "Now that you mention it, I do believe my father said something about that. What sort of science are you interested in?"

"At the moment? The science of the mind." Ewan studied her face for her reaction.

"The mind?" She frowned. "What do you mean?"

"I've read quite a bit of research on the human brain. It's capable of much more than we know, but it also can be injured in ways we aren't aware of."

"Yes. I know." Thea nodded, turning quiet. "My mother's brain was injured."

Ewan nearly dropped his fork. "It was?"

Thea nodded again.

"If you don't mind my asking, what happened to her?" he prompted, hoping he hadn't made her feel uncomfortable with his question. Why did they always seem to end up speaking of such things?

"My mother loved to ride. It was her most treasured pastime." Thea traced her fingertip along the base of her wine glass. "The reason Mama was sick was because she was thrown from a horse. She hit her head quite soundly. The doctors guessed her brain was bleeding. She didn't speak for months, well over a year. She slowly wasted away."

"And that's when you took care of her?" Ewan prompted.

Thea nodded. "Yes. She couldn't speak. Could barely write. But we managed to communicate."

A lump formed in Ewan's throat. "That must have been extremely difficult for you."

"I loved my mother very much," she replied, glancing away.

Ewan was left to wonder if that same sentiment extended to her father.

"I took care of Mama for the better part of two years. She died just a few days after my eighteenth birthday."

A tug of pity pulled at Ewan's heartstrings. What an awful time for a girl to lose her mother. Thea had lost her mother at the same time she would have been preparing to make her debut in Society. An awful thought struck him. "Was that why you didn't have a debut? Is that why you didn't marry?"

Thea's gaze swung back to her plate. "Yes, that was why. I was in mourning and even though Father attempted to cut our mourning short in order for me to attend the events of the Season, I refused. And I refused to go the next year also." Thea shook her head.

"Understandable," Ewan replied softly. "So, your mother died from the injury to her brain then?"

Thea's nostrils flared. "I didn't say that. Mama wasted away from a brain injury. She died because she no longer had the will to live. I'm certain she could have recovered if she'd wanted to."

Ewan could tell from the anger in her voice that Thea didn't want to discuss what she meant by those words. He would not push her.

Thea shook her head and a smile popped to her lips. "At any rate, that's enough of that talk." She took another sip of wine. "What other sort of science are you interested in?"

Ewan was glad for the change of subject. The last thing he wanted to do was to make Thea sad again or bring up unhappy thoughts. "All sorts of things," he replied, "like the best sorts of crop rotations and inventing a brace for a wheelchair." He grinned at her. "But I've also talked to Edward Jenner about his *vaccinae*, for example."

Thea's brows shot up. "You've spoken to *Edward Jenner*? Himself?"

"You're familiar with Jenner?" Ewan couldn't help the surprise in his voice. He'd never met a female who'd heard of Jenner.

"Of course I've heard of him. Why, I've even read *Inquiry into the Variolae Vaccinae Known as the Cow Pox*. His concept that the *vaccinae* could prevent smallpox was nothing short of brilliant."

Ewan stared at her again as if she was some sort of magical being. "I quite agree."

"You do, however, realize that while Jenner may have invented the *vaccinae*, he wasn't the first to come up with the concept." Thea gave him a placating smile.

Ewan frowned. "He wasn't?"

"No, actually," Thea continued. "That distinction belongs to Lady Mary Wortley Montagu, who brought it back to England last century from the *women* of the Ottoman empire. Jenner was treated with her revelation as a child."

Ewan's brows shot up. "Is that so?"

"Yes, though I suppose I shouldn't be shocked to learn you didn't know that, given that you're surprised a woman even knew about it, let alone invented it in the first place." She blinked at him innocently, her smile still firmly in place.

Ewan inclined his head toward her and chuckled. "My apologies, my lady. You're completely right, of course. Point taken."

Thea waved her hand in the air. "Of course, I've also read Jenner's paper on *angina pectoris*. His theory on the coronary arteries is quite fascinating as well."

"You seem to be interested in medicine," Ewan asked, eyeing her carefully again.

Thea glanced down at her plate. "I had to be."

"Why is that?" Ewan took a bite of his mackerel.

Thea dabbed at her lips with her napkin. "When my mother was sick, I read all I could in the medical field to understand what might be wrong with her. Hoping to find something that could help."

Ewan eyed Thea over the top of his wine glass. Last night he'd realized that he'd misjudged her. Tonight, he realized that he had not only misjudged her, he had *sorely* underestimated the lady. She was witty and well-read, her closest friend was a maid, and she'd spent her time sewing a nightrail for one of his servants as a thank-you gift. This was all in addition to what he already knew, which was that she'd spent some of the most important years of her life caring for her invalid mother when she could have easily left that task to servants.

Far from her temperament being the reason she was a spinster, as he'd so uncharitably guessed when he met her, Thea had given up her marriage prospects to care for her ailing mother. Instead of going to parties and buying new frocks, she'd been busy reading about medical science and educating herself in an attempt to save her mother's life. Thea was far from the spoiled pampered princess he'd assumed to her be when she'd refused to stop sneaking into his stables.

Ewan drained his glass. He couldn't remember the last time he'd been so wrong about someone. The fact that Thea's mother had had a brain injury and Thea had tended to her for months was certainly a revelation as well. She obviously had patience and was caring if she was able to do that. Phillip's injury was quite similar. In addition to being shot, he'd been thrown from his horse and hit his head.

For the first time since Thea had arrived, Ewan began to wonder if he could actually share his secret with her. Would she be willing to help? Could he trust her to tell her about Phillip?

# CHAPTER NINETEEN

"Please, Mag, open the door. I need your help." Thea sat in her wheelchair directly behind her bedchamber door the next morning, staring at the thing as if it were an immovable boulder. It was the only thing that sat between herself and freedom. With the help of Maggie and Giles, she'd got into her wheelchair and propped up her leg. Now she wanted out of the room to go exploring. For one purpose and one purpose only. To find out who Clayton was hiding down the hall.

Dinner last night had been even more revealing than the night before. Specifically, Lord Clayton had revealed himself to be a man who did not believe that women knew much about medicine, that was for certain. Thea could almost laugh at the thought if it weren't so aggravating. She'd demonstrated just how much she'd known, however, during their discussion of Edward Jenner. She could tell by the look on Ewan's face that he'd been impressed with her knowledge.

As for what *she'd* revealed last night, somehow the blasted viscount had got her to talk even more openly about her mother. Other than Maggie and Anthony, who both knew everything, Ewan was the only person Thea had ever told about her mother's sadness. There was something about the way the man seemed to intently listen and to truly care that made her answer any question he asked.

The truth was that the doctors had believed her mother could have made a full recovery. But Thea knew something the doctors didn't. Mama had been out riding Helena in the rain the morning of her accident because Father had left again for London, and his mistress.

Thea would never forget her mother's words to her the night before. Wearing her nightrail, Thea had gone to Mama's bedchamber to kiss her cheek and say goodnight as she always did.

Mama had looked so sad and pale. Her eyes were swollen, and she'd obviously been crying. Mama had recently told sixteen-year-old Thea the story of how Papa had a mistress in London. She'd had to explain to her what a mistress was. Thea had been aghast. She had little doubt that's why Mama was crying.

"Did Papa make you cry again?" Thea had asked, placing a hand on her mother's thin shoulder.

Mama had turned to Thea and grabbed her hand. "Listen to me, Thea. Don't ever marry a man who doesn't love you back. It's pure torture."

Thea had nodded at her mother, her eyes wide. Her throat had been too dry to reply. She hated seeing her mother that way, but she didn't know what to say to comfort her.

"I mean it, Thea," Mama had continued. "I've seen to it that you'll have enough money to live on should you need it without marrying. You mustn't be forced into it. Your father is leaving again tonight. To go back to London. Back to *her*. You won't have to live a life like I've had to. You must marry a man who loves you undeniably."

Swallowing the lump in her throat, Thea had nodded, kissed her mother, and left the room. Thea remembered seeing her father coming out of the adjoining bedchamber, two footmen scurrying in front of him carrying his trunks.

She glared at her father.

"Take care of your mother, Theodora," the man had had the audacity to say.

Thea had lifted her chin. She understood precisely where her father was going and why. "I take better care of her than you do," Thea had whispered.

Her father had merely continued on his way.

The next morning, Mama had gone out in the rain to ride Helena hell-for-leather across the pastures. She'd taken a path she normally didn't take and attempted a jump she normally wouldn't have attempted. She'd nearly broken her neck.

Upon hearing the news that his wife had been so grievously injured, Father hadn't even bothered to return to Devon to check on her. Instead, he'd written a letter to Thea, asking her to give her *his best*.

From that day forward, Thea had treated her father like a stranger. She'd seen him briefly from time to time in the nearly two years her mother was sick, but he always left for London as soon as he'd finished any business at home.

He visited mother sparingly and hadn't bothered to see her at all the last time he left before she died. According to the doctors, Mama had died of a lingering brain injury resulting from the fall from her horse two years earlier. But Thea knew better. Her Mama had died from a broken heart.

"I refuse to encourage you in sneaking about this house, putting your nose into affairs that have nothing to do with you," Maggie said, pulling Thea from her unhappy memories.

Maggie was across the room, folding some of Thea's garments and placing them in the wardrobe. Thea turned her head toward the maid with an impatient sigh. "Don't you want to know who Lord Clayton is hiding in the next wing?"

Thea hadn't got far with Ewan last night. When she'd questioned him, he'd acted as if there was nowhere she couldn't venture in the house. She guessed that was because he didn't want to appear suspicious, and he most likely had no inkling that she would begin poking around bedchambers to find his (other) hidden guest.

Exactly how many people was the man hiding in this house? For all she knew, there were more than two. He certainly had seemed as if he had nothing to hide. If there was another house guest, why wasn't that guest invited to dinner also? Perhaps Rosalie was mistaken. Or perhaps, Ewan was simply a good liar. There was only one way to find out. She intended to go poking into bedchambers, as soon as she could get out of *this* blasted one.

"No, I don't want to know who Lord Clayton is hiding in the next wing," Maggie replied firmly. "And you shouldn't either. In fact, you should be much more concerned with the fact that the same maid who told you *that* secret may be telling other people *your* secret. She's obviously a secret teller."

Thea froze. "Good heavens, you're right. I didn't even think about that." She bit her lip and considered her friend's words for a few moments. "That *is* something to worry about, isn't it?"

"Yes. It is. And the reason you didn't think of it before now is because you're too busy being meddlesome," Maggie replied.

"I cannot help being curious. Besides, what else am I to do, trapped in this house? I cannot believe Anthony hasn't at least written yet." Thea would have stamped her foot if she hadn't been sitting in a wheelchair with one leg propped up.

Maggie blinked at her over the top of the bed sheet she

was folding. "I thought you were hoping he'd arrive instead of write."

"I *am*, but at this point I'd welcome a letter. What in the world could be keeping him?" Thea had maneuvered herself close enough to the door to tug at the handle, but the angle she was at would ensure that the door could not open wide enough for her to push herself into the corridor. "Please Maggie, help me."

Maggie sighed and stalked to the door. She waited with her hands on her hips for Thea to move herself far enough away from the door to open it. Once it was open, Thea gleefully pedaled herself into the corridor. "Thank you," she called. "I'll be back later."

"You're supposed to be hiding," Maggie replied in a half-whisper.

"Very few servants are allowed on this floor. Rosalie told me herself," Thea shot back.

"Yes, let's believe whatever Rosalie says. Including the fact that there's another guest hidden up here somewhere."

Over her shoulder, Thea gave her friend a wicked smile. "There's only one way to find out."

"I know my words are about to fall on deaf ears, but it's none of your business if Lord Clayton is housing another guest on this property. You should leave it alone."

Thea took off in the direction of the far end of the corridor. "You know me, Maggie. There's no possible way I'm going to leave it alone."

～

"My lady, wake up," came Maggie's voice through Thea's sleepy haze.

Thea shook herself awake and glanced around. She was sitting in a corner of a corridor in her wheelchair and she'd clearly been asleep for some time. "What time is it?" she groggily asked the maid who was smiling down at her, her arms folded over her chest.

"Nearly four o'clock," was Maggie's reply.

"In the afternoon?" Thea asked. Where was she? And what had she been do— She glanced around and searched her memory. "Lord Clayton's houseguest. I never found her."

"By the looks of things, you didn't get too far," Maggie replied. "You're only around the corner from your own room."

"What? What happened? I feel asleep?" Thea shook her groggy head, still not fully comprehending what happened.

"Laudanum will do that to a person," Maggie replied in a singsong voice.

"Laudanum? But I didn't have any laud—" Thea sat up straighter and glared at the maid. "My tea! Margaret Mary Hill, you put laudanum in my tea this morning, didn't you? I knew it had a strange taste."

"I warned you to mind your own affairs," Maggie replied, shrugging.

"You know how I am," Thea insisted, trying desperately to back her chair from the corner.

"Yes, I do, which is precisely why I put laudanum in your tea. Now, I'm taking you back to your bedchamber to begin preparing for dinner. Lord Clayton has asked that you join him in the dining room once again."

# CHAPTER TWENTY

After the footmen had cleared away dinner that evening, Ewan dismissed them both. Then he wheeled Thea into the drawing room directly off of the dining room and shut the doors so none of the passing servants would see them.

He pushed Thea's chair next to the settee where he took a seat. They'd had another fine meal, talking and laughing, sharing bits of information they knew about others in the area and joking about everything from horse racing to Shakespeare's plays.

Ewan was thoroughly impressed with Lady Thea Ballard. She was proving to be witty, warm, and quite clever. She obviously loved her brother a great deal, loved Alabaster perhaps more, and was somewhat tepid when it came to her father. Her mother, however, was someone she had loved quite fiercely. It was tragic that the lady had been taken from her young daughter so soon.

Ewan stood and walked to the sideboard. "Would you care for some port?"

"No, thank you. I don't think alcohol and laudanum mix very well," Thea replied.

Ewan chuckled. He poured himself a glass of port and returned to sit next to Thea on the settee. They were merely a foot's length apart.

Thea turned to stare at Ewan, blinking rapidly. "I… I have something important that I want to say. Well, ask, really."

Ewan frowned. "Yes?" he prompted.

She cleared her throat and folded her hands, placing them primly in her lap. "I want to…admit to something. Something I'm not terribly proud of."

Dread began to spread through Ewan's middle. "What is it?"

"I was going to sneak around and look myself, but I've decided that did me no favors last time—well, that and I've got a maid who'd sooner drug me than allow me to be meddlesome. At any rate, I've decided to come right out with it." She blinked at him some more.

Now that she was so close, he realized that she had the loveliest longest eyelashes. He continued to eye her warily, however. "Out with what?"

Thea straightened her shoulders and met his gaze directly. Quite disconcerting. Quite. "Who are you hiding in the other wing of the house?"

Ewan nearly spit the sip of port he'd just taken. "What?"

"You have another houseguest, do you not?"

"Who told you that?" He was forced to wipe his mouth with the back of his hand.

Thea let her gaze drop. "I overheard some servants talking."

"Which servants?" He eyed her warily again.

"It doesn't matter. It's clearly true or you wouldn't be so upset," she replied, meeting his gaze once again. "Now, will you tell me, or must I investigate on my own?"

Ewan set his port glass on the table in front of him. The young woman couldn't help herself. She'd only been able to act properly for two nights. Now she was back to being completely improper. Ewan wasn't thrilled that one of the servants had been gossiping about Phillip to Thea, but the truth was, he'd already considered telling her about him. He expelled a deep breath. "Let me ask you something, Lady Thea."

She had an impatient look on her face, but she nodded.

Ewan smoothed his hand down his shirtfront while he spoke. "If the other guest knew you were there, would you want that guest to come looking for *you?*"

Thea wrinkled her nose. Clearly, she didn't appreciate his logic. "I suppose I would not," she finally said.

She'd been honest. That was big of her. He'd been half expecting her to deny it. "Well, then, don't you think you should give my other guest the courtesy of staying in privacy?"

Thea blinked at him again. She was nodding. "I know I should do that, but I'm afraid I'm overwhelmed with curiosity and I cannot stand it."

Ewan laughed and shook his head. "You're honest, I'll give you that."

"Father says I'm honest to a fault." She sighed. "But not as often as Father says I'm stubborn to a fault."

"That I know firsthand to be true," Ewan replied. "I suppose me asking you not to try to find out who my other guest is will do no good?"

Thea had the most adorable guilty look on her face as she raised her pretty gray eyes to meet his. "I could promise you I wouldn't, my lord, but I'm afraid I would break my promise within hours."

Ewan shook his head again. "Very well. Then it's probably

a good thing that I was already considering telling you about him."

"Him?" Her eyes went wide.

"Yes," Ewan chuckled again. "You didn't truly think I had more than one young lady hiding in the wings, did you?"

Thea smiled. "Honestly, I had no idea. I have a vivid imagination, you see, so I had many different guesses."

"Please, don't tell me any of them. You might shock me."

Thea inclined her head. "I'm afraid I would, honestly."

Ewan leaned closer to her and whispered. They were so close their breath mingled. "The truth is that I was planning to ask for your help where my other guest is concerned."

"My help? How could I possibly help?" she whispered back.

Ewan was so close he could see the tiny trace of freckles along the bridge of her nose. He was tempted to reach out and touch the soft skin of her cheek. He shook himself to clear his head of such thoughts. "The other guest is my friend, Phillip. He's been staying here for several months. He's not quite himself at the moment."

Thea's chest rose and fell with each breath. Ewan couldn't help but notice her enticing *décolletage*.

"What do you mean?" she breathed.

"He's a soldier. In addition to some other injuries he sustained in the war, he has a brain injury. From being thrown by a horse." He paused and watched as Thea digested that bit of information.

"I'm sorry to hear that," she breathed.

"He hasn't spoken since he arrived."

Thea's slight gasp made the hair on the back of Ewan's neck stand up. "I'm sorry to hear that," she whispered.

"I was hoping—"

"You were hoping I might be able to help, given my experience with my mother?" she finished for him.

He nodded once. "I understand if you don't want to. It's a lot to ask."

"Not at all. I'd be happy to help. It's the least I can do after you've been so kind as to allow me to stay here. But I do have one question."

"What's that?" Ewan asked.

"I can understand you wanting to help your friend who was injured in war, but what I can't understand is...why is it all such a secret?"

# CHAPTER TWENTY-ONE

Thea watched as a range of emotions played across Ewan's face. There was surprise, there was regret, and there was…indecision.

When he finally spoke, he said, "Did you know there's quite a bit of scientific theory on the effect of animals on the mind of those who've experienced shock?"

"Yes, actually," Thea replied, confusion marring her brow. What did this have to do with the secrecy surrounding Phillip? "There is a man on the continent who is an expert on the subject. I wanted to try to send for him when Mother was ill, but Father refused. His name is Forrester, I believe."

Ewan expelled his breath. "Would you believe me if I told you that Mr. Forrester is here?"

Thea's eyes widened. "What? Truly?"

"Yes, he's been working with Phillip for a several days now."

"But…why?" Thea asked.

Ewan turned to her. "You asked me why Phillip being here is a secret. I know it seems odd. But there is a good reason. You see, Phillip isn't just a soldier."

Thea held her breath. "Who is he?"

"He's the rightful Duke of Harlowe."

Thea's eyes shot open wide. "What?"

Ewan nodded again. "That's correct."

Thea lowered her voice to a whisper and leaned closer to Ewan. "The rightful Duke of Harlowe? The old duke's second son? But I thought he was dead."

Ewan nodded slowly. "Everyone thinks he's dead. But he didn't die at war. He was put on a ship back to England and my friend, the Marquess of Bellingham, found him. Phillip was nothing like his former self."

Thea took a shuddering breath, trying to assimilate the news. "So that means…"

"Alabaster was his horse. They were at war together."

Thea nodded as tears stung the backs of her eyes. In a hundred years, she would never have guessed that Ewan had wanted to win Alabaster to give him back to a man who had nearly lost his life.

Thea listened silently and carefully as Ewan spent the next several minutes telling her the story of how Phillip had saved *his* life.

"And so, when Bell wrote to me from Dover telling me a ship had just arrived with injured soldiers from the Continent and one of them was Phillip, I made haste to the shore to gather him. I brought him here and he's been here since. His brother had already died by then and it wasn't clear whether he was aware of it."

Ewan was still within an arm's length of her when Thea leaned even closer and whispered. "So, you owed your friend your life and in return you've taken him in at his darkest hour?"

"Precisely," Ewan replied, his gaze locked with hers.

"That's why you had to buy Alabaster," she breathed.

"Yes." Ewan nodded.

"And that's why it's a secret that Phillip is here," she continued.

Ewan nodded again. "Yes, and I must ask you to keep it a secret."

She nodded sagely. "Of course I will keep it a secret. But the entire *ton* thinks he's dead," she whispered. "Why wouldn't he want to declare himself right away?"

"There are a few reasons," Ewan replied, "but the most important at the moment is that he's not yet ready to take his place in Society. He isn't strong enough."

Suddenly, it all made sense. The secrecy. Ewan's need to buy the horse at any price. Mr. Forrester being here, all of it. Thea tried to remember. Had she ever met Phillip before? The second son of the Duke of Harlowe? She couldn't recall such a meeting, but perhaps it had taken place when she was younger.

"It must be difficult for Phillip," she finally said, turning her head toward Ewan. "He's been so ill, *and* his brother died."

"Precisely." Ewan rubbed the back of his neck. "He needs a bit more time. To heal."

"It's completely understandable," Thea replied, nodding. She felt nothing but compassion for the poor soldier who no doubt had the weight of the world on his back now.

Ewan's gaze met hers. "I must have your word that you will tell no one that Phillip is here. Or that he's alive for that matter. It's quite important."

"You have it, of course," she replied, pleased that he trusted her enough to share such a secret.

He leaned toward her and for a dizzying moment, Thea thought he was going to kiss her. First, he'd trusted her with his largest secret, now he was going to kiss her. And she wanted him too. She closed her eyes, ready, so ready.

His lips barely brushed her cheek. A shudder raced down

her spine as he whispered in her ear, "Thank you, Thea." Then, he pulled away.

Thea wanted to sob.

# CHAPTER TWENTY-TWO

The next morning, Thea prepared herself to meet
Phillip. Ewan had asked her to meet his friend
today and she had readily agreed. Maggie had
already helped her dress and Thea was sitting in her wheelchair staring out the windows of her bedchamber, thinking
about last night, and Ewan.

Her mind raced whenever she thought about their
conversation last night. They'd been close enough to kiss. In
fact, she'd had the thought more than once that he was going
to kiss her and worse, she'd thought more than twice that
she'd *like* it if he did. She'd been *hoping* that he would kiss
her. Only he hadn't. And Thea was left to wonder if she were
going mad. Why was she having thoughts about Lord Clayton...Ewan kissing her? It was madness, was it not? Could
she blame it on the laudanum?

She'd spent the night tossing and turning in bed—as
much as her broken leg allowed—thinking on it. Ewan was a
gentleman. He wasn't about to kiss her. It would be
completely improper. Oh, did he even want to kiss her? She

thought she'd read it in his eyes, but perhaps she was being ridiculous. Perhaps it hadn't been a spark of longing that had leaped between them as they'd whispered together after dinner. Perhaps he had merely been doing his best to keep his friend's identity a secret.

And he'd told her the secret. That said something. Oh, she may have heard about it and asked, but she could tell he'd been telling the truth when he'd told her that he'd already been planning on asking for her help. The look in his eyes had been sincere.

Her heart hurt when she thought about Phillip, the injured soldier, the would-be duke, who hadn't spoken a word in months. Just like Mama. Phillip had basically been trapped in his rooms here. She'd never seen him leave. In fact, she probably never would have seen him at all unless she'd gone knocking on his door.

She had to admit that it felt good to know that Ewan trusted her enough to tell her such an important secret. The intrusive young woman he'd met the night she'd broken her leg in his stables would never have wrestled a secret from him. She knew that much to be true.

Meanwhile, she had yet to hear from her brother. She had written Anthony two more letters and hadn't received a single reply. It was unlike him to ignore her. She was beginning to wonder if he'd taken ill, or perhaps he'd gone to London and the letters hadn't caught up to him yet. But it had been days. Surely, he would have received *one* of them by now.

A knock on her door startled her from her thoughts. "Come in," she called, smoothing a hand down her middle.

The door opened and Ewan stepped inside. "Good morning, my lady." He bowed.

"Good morning, my lord." She inclined her head to him in return.

He was dressed in buff-colored breeches and a dark blue coat with a white shirtfront. His snowy cravat was tied negligently about his neck. Black boots completed his ensemble. Why did the man have to be *so* handsome? And he *was* handsome. She'd thought so before she'd had any laudanum.

"Are you ready to meet Phillip?" Ewan asked next.

"Yes, indeed." She shook her head in an attempt to clear it of thoughts of Ewan's hooded blue eyes, his wide shoulders, and his—

Ewan stepped behind her and began pushing her chair toward the door. Giles, who had been waiting in the hall, held the door open and allowed Ewan and Thea to enter the corridor.

Ewan turned to the left and pushed the chair all the way down the long corridor, past a turn, and down another long corridor to the other wing of the house. Apparently, Rosalie had been correct. Phillip was hidden away in his own wing.

"Phillip has a set of rooms," Ewan explained as they went. "A bedchamber, a dressing room, and a sitting room. I'm taking you to the sitting room, of course."

Thea nodded. She was looking forward to meeting Phillip, but she had to wonder…was he confined to bed? Was he comatose? Ewan hadn't mentioned details of his friend's illness.

When they came to the end of the second long corridor, Ewan stopped in front of the first of three remaining doors. He cleared his throat before knocking. There was no answer. They waited for several seconds before Ewan said, "I always give him a bit of time before entering."

Thea nodded.

Giles, who had accompanied them, opened the door and Ewan pushed Thea's chair inside.

If Thea was expecting a dark, dank room filled with the smells of ether and laudanum, what she found instead was a brightly lit room with the curtains pulled back from huge windows and everything in place, orderly and freshly cleaned. While her own rooms were decorated in a decidedly feminine fashion, Phillip's rooms were masculine with dark blue finishes and paintings of foxes and hounds. It was all as finely appointed as her own room, and the scent of lemon wax and starch hung in the air.

After her eyes adjusted to the bright sunlight streaming through the lovely sitting room, she finally saw Phillip. Far from being confined to a bed, he was dressed impeccably in buff-colored breeches, a blue coat and white waistcoat, and white shirtfront and cravat. His clothing looked much like Ewan's. Phillip wore black boots and was sitting at a table, staring out the window. He looked perfectly healthy, but Thea knew better.

At Ewan and Thea's entrance, Phillip turned his head. From across the room, Thea couldn't exactly tell, but she thought she saw a flicker of something—what?—flash through his eyes. Was he surprised to see another a guest, a female at that? Had Ewan told him she was coming?

While Ewan rolled her chair to the other side of the table, Giles rushed ahead and moved the existing chair out of the way so Ewan could push Thea's seat up to take the space.

"Phillip," intoned Ewan in a subdued, even tone. "May I introduce you to Lady Theodora Ballard. She is a neighbor."

Phillip stared silently at Thea and she inclined her head to him.

Ewan barely paused. "Lady Thea, this is my friend, Phillip. He's a captain in His Majesty's army."

Thea acted as if receiving no surname during an intro-duction was perfectly normal. But she and Ewan had agreed that Thea would not mention Phillip's family or his future title. "A pleasure to meet you, Sir," she said.

"I thought you might enjoy a lady's company for a change, Phillip," Ewan said next. He turned to grab the chair and sit with them when Thea lifted a finger to stop him.

"I hate to be rude, my lord," she said to Ewan, "but will you please leave us alone?"

# CHAPTER TWENTY-THREE

After the door shut behind Ewan, Thea rolled herself even closer to the small table that separated her from Phillip. She leaned across the table as best she could, placing her arms atop it and contemplated Ewan's other house guest.

Phillip had dark blond hair and green eyes. He was certainly young and handsome, but pain was obvious in the lines on his face. The man had been hurt, and not just physically. The slightest start of wrinkles touched the corners of his eyes and anguish was etched on either side of his mouth. He was too thin, and he looked quite…unhappy. Her heart immediately went out to him. Here was a man who was lost. The thought came out of nowhere. She immediately resolved to befriend him.

She leaned forward and in a conspiratorial whisper, she said, "It's nice to meet you, Phillip. I just discovered last night that Lord Clayton has more than one patient hidden in his house. Why, the man is practically running a secret hospital."

Phillip blinked at her and remained silent, but she could have sworn she saw the flicker of humor on his face.

She watched him expectantly for a few moments before shrugging and saying, "It seems you and I are in somewhat of the same boat at the moment. That is to say, we're both guests of Lord Clayton while we recuperate. As you can see, I have broken my leg. The details of which I shall spare you. But I will say that it happened under excruciatingly embarrassing circumstances. Quite a tale, I assure you. Perhaps a story for another day if you're feeling up to it sometime."

She stared at him expectantly again. He stared calmly and silently back. The man might be ill, but he was certainly not comatose as she'd feared. He was awake, alert, and staring directly at her. Whatever was wrong with him, she had the distinct feeling that the reason he wasn't speaking was entirely by choice, not because he lacked the ability. *That* was interesting.

She tried to get him to speak by enticing him with the story about how she'd come to be a guest here. That hadn't done it. She needed something more compelling. She glanced about. She needed something interesting enough to get him to ask questions.

"Lord Clayton told me that your stay here should remain a secret, and you have my word that I shall keep it. But I must tell you…I have a secret too."

THEA SPENT the next fortnight convinced that her brother had either abandoned her entirely or was dead. Meanwhile she had breakfast with Phillip every day. Her mention of a secret had not enticed him to speak that first morning, but that didn't stop her from trying something new each day. The second day Phillip said nothing while she spoke at great length about her life at her Father's house. The third day he said nothing while she spoke at great length about Maggie and all the antics they'd got up to together over the years. The fourth day he said nothing while she spoke at great length of her mother and Anthony. The fifth, sixth, and seventh days, Phillip remained completely silent while she told him the details of her stay at Clayton Manor. The eighth through the thirteenth day, Phillip watched her quietly as she showed him the tricks she'd learned regarding how to maneuver her wheelchair.

It wasn't until the fourteenth day that she spoke of Alabaster. And it was after discussing the matter with Mr. Forrester, whom she'd met at dinner with Ewan the night before.

Thea waited until breakfast had been served and the footmen had retreated to stand near the wall. "Remember the day we met, I mentioned I had a secret to tell?" Thea began.

Phillip stared at her silently as usual.

"Well, you're obviously too much of a gentleman to ask," she continued, "but I'll tell you just the same." She took a deep breath. "You see, I deserved to break my leg."

She stared at him expectantly for a few moments before continuing. "The truth is that I sneaked into Lord Clayton's stables not once but *three times*." She paused to see if that would elicit a reaction, but Phillip just blinked at her. "*In the middle of the night*." Another pause.

Nothing.

"I had a very good reason to, of course," Thea continued. "You see, Lord Clayton stole my horse." She glanced at Phillip again, hoping that strange-sounding bit of news might finally convince him to speak.

"All right, very well. He didn't *steal* my horse. He won it, at auction. But I'd sent my brother to buy the horse and Lord Clayton had the audacity to bid a ridiculously high amount of money. A small fortune, I tell you."

Phillip just stared at her.

"He's the most beautiful horse in the world, however. An Arabian, from the finest bloodline. His name is Alabaster."

Phillip's head snapped up and a ragged sound emerged from his throat. He cleared it and tried again. "Alabaster," he said in a rough whisper.

Her heart pounding, Thea nodded and smiled. She wanted to laugh and clap her hands, but she knew she needed to remain calm. "Yes. Alabaster. I understand that you know him too. He's living in Lord Clayton's stables. You should go visit him sometime."

"Alabaster," came Phillip's whisper again.

"Would you like to see him?" Thea prompted. She reached out and patted Phillip's hand that lay on the table in front of him.

He nodded.

Thea nodded too. She knew from speaking to Mr. Forrester that she should leave well enough alone for the day. The fact that Phillip had actually uttered a word, not once but *twice* was a huge accomplishment. He would no doubt be strained and tired afterward. She should make her excuses and leave so he could rest.

"Excellent," she said, drawing back her hand. "Let's plan to go out to the stables and visit him one day this week."

A sharp rap on the door interrupted them. "Come in," Thea called knowing it could only be one of the servants who knew they were there or Ewan himself.

Maggie came rushing in the door. A look of relief washed over her face when she saw Thea sitting at the table under the window. "There you are my lady. I'm awfully sorry to bother you, but you've just received a letter and I knew you'd want to read it immediately. It's from your brother."

# CHAPTER TWENTY-FOUR

"**H**e's not coming to get me!" Thea announced in a voice that was rising with panic. Her hands shook as she held her brother's letter. Thea had quickly made excuses to Phillip and rushed back to her room where she could read her letter in private.

Maggie made her way to Thea's side and hovered over her shoulder to look at the letter. "What do you mean he's not coming to get you?"

Thea scanned the letter again to ensure she hadn't misread. She *had* to have misread. There was no possible way Anthony would ignore her pleas to take her home and leave her here to rot. She'd been half convinced he was ill or dead. Now that she knew he was perfectly fine and purposefully ignoring her, she was incensed. She'd already been here for over a fortnight. According to Dr. Blanchard she may have to remain for up to *four more* weeks. Anthony couldn't possibly leave her here all that time.

"Here, you read it." She thrust the letter toward Maggie. Maggie grabbed the missive and swiftly read aloud.

*Dearest Thea,*

*I hope this letter finds you well and that your leg is healing properly. As to that, Father has informed me of the dire circumstances involved if we were to move you in your current condition. I visited Dr. Blanchard in town myself and he has confirmed what Father said. I have stayed away and not paid you a visit as I'm told that you're in the house secretively and not accepting visitors. I look forward to seeing you when you return. Please do not be cross with me.*

*Yours most sincerely,*

*Anthony*

Thea grabbed the letter from Maggie and glared at the offensive thing. "'Please do not be cross with me,'" she mimicked. "What other way would I be? Why? Why would he do this to me? I explained the situation to him. I told him he could be ruined. Father could be ruined. Does he not care? I even wrote him and explained there's a maid who knows I'm here and is a blatant secret-teller. I even told him you'd resorted to drugging me."

"I only drugged you once," Maggie pointed out, rolling her eyes. "Besides, your brother is worried about your leg."

Thea's voice raised an octave. "He should be worried about my reputation. And his!"

"I agree with you, Thea, but if Anthony won't come, it seems you're out of options."

Thea feverishly glanced around the room. "I am never out of options as long as my brain is functioning. Get me a quill and some vellum. If Anthony refuses to come to my rescue, I shall just have to write to Uncle Teddy in London. *He'll* be worried about my reputation. I'm certain of it."

## CHAPTER TWENTY-FIVE

Ewan paused outside Phillip's door. He'd been about to knock, but he could have sworn he heard a man's voice coming from inside. A man's voice talking and...laughing? No. That couldn't possibly be true. He listened for a few more moments and heard it again. First, the sound of Thea's bright voice met his ears and then a voice he hadn't heard in years—Phillip's voice—replying in kind with a definite chuckle.

Had Thea somehow managed the impossible and persuaded Phillip to speak after only a fortnight with him? Ewan had to find out for certain. He knocked quickly and then entered the room. Thea was sitting in her wheelchair near the windows. Phillip was sitting at a small table near her and they were in fact, smiling.

Their gazes swung to Ewan.

"Good morning," Ewan muttered, feeling like a complete horse's arse for barging in on their private discussion.

"Good morning, Lord Clayton," Thea replied with a bright smile. "It's a lovely day, isn't it?"

Ewan's gaze remained locked on Phillip. His friend tipped his head to the side and said, "Good morning, Clayton."

Ewan swallowed the lump in his throat. Phillip had just spoken his first words to him in all these months.

"How are you feeling?" Ewan continued. The idiotic question seemed to burst from his mouth.

"I'm feeling quite fit," Thea replied, still grinning. "And I'd venture to say Phillip is too. Aren't you, Phillip?"

Phillip nodded. "Indeed, I am, Lady Thea."

Ewan's gaze flipped back and forth between the two of them. He stared at them both in wonder. They were acting as if this were any other day and nothing at all was amiss. Well, Ewan wasn't about to put an end to the camaraderie. He, too, intended to act as if this was normal. He didn't want Phillip to feel uncomfortable.

"In fact," Thea continued, "Phillip was just saying that he would like to see Alabaster now."

Ewan wasted no time scrambling to get both Thea and Phillip out to the stables. He employed both trusted footmen to help carry Thea and her wheelchair out. Phillip walked alongside them.

The moment Phillip entered the stables he made his way to Alabaster's stall. He petted the horse and spoke to him softly. He rubbed Alabaster's head, petted his nose, and fed him an apple.

Ewan quietly pushed Thea's chair to the far side of a nearby stall to give Phillip and the horse time to reacquaint themselves.

As soon as Ewan stopped the wheelchair, Thea said, "Help me to stand, please. I want to watch Phillip and Alabaster together."

Ewan quickly complied, offering his arm to Thea as she pushed her way to stand on her good leg. Then he lifted her carefully in his arms and set her down next to the stall railing. Thea leaned against the thick wooden rail for support. She was able to see Phillip and Alabaster from there.

"I must admit that you've amazed me, Thea," Ewan said moments later as he watched Phillip yards away petting the fine horse.

"Amazed you?" she replied with a laugh. "How?"

"You've done what I could not do. You've somehow managed to convince Phillip to speak and to leave his bedchamber."

"I didn't do much. Phillip was ready to do those things. You've taken excellent care of him, Ewan."

"He hasn't said a word for months. Not until you began meeting with him."

"Do you want to know the truth?" Thea asked.

"By all means."

"I don't think Phillip's injury was physical as much as mental," Thea replied.

Ewan frowned. "Why do you say that?"

"I've spoken to Mr. Forrester. If Phillip's brain had been damaged, he may not have been able to speak when he chose. I think he was merely waiting for the right time. My presence has provided that."

Ewan frowned. "What do you mean?"

"When my mother was sick, I could tell she *wanted* to talk, but she couldn't. She couldn't form the words. Phillip's problem wasn't like that. He *could* talk. He was just choosing not to. I think he was coping with the things he'd seen at war. I've asked him about those things."

Ewan sucked in his breath. "He told you?"

"A little. Some of it. It seems quite painful for him to remember it."

They both looked back over to where Phillip was quietly speaking to Alabaster. Then Ewan returned his gaze to Thea. Tears shone in her eyes. "You're crying," he said softly, pulling his handkerchief from his coat pocket and handing it to her.

"Yes." She wiped away the tears with the cloth. "But not for the reason you think."

He smiled at that. "What do you think I think?"

Thea dabbed at her eyes with the handkerchief. "That I'm crying because I can't have Alabaster."

"I don't think that, Thea. But why *are* you crying?"

She lifted her chin toward Phillip and Alabaster. "I'm crying because they obviously love each other. If I had known that you had purchased Alabaster for Phillip, I wouldn't have been so hellbent on getting him back for myself."

Ewan shook his head. "You couldn't have known that Thea. Besides, you had Alabaster when he was a foal. He means a lot to you."

She nodded. "Yes, but Phillip explained to me how closely they bonded during the war. He and Alabaster were partners."

"I knew Alabaster meant a great deal to him," Ewan breathed. "That's why money was not an object when I bid for him."

"And my brother ramped up the bidding," Thea said, shaking her head.

"Ballard had no way to know why I wanted to win the horse so badly. Just as I had no way of knowing how badly you wanted him."

Thea expelled her breath. "Well, even if I could, I wouldn't take Alabaster away from Phillip now. He needs him. He needs him more than I do."

Ewan took a deep breath. "That's really quite generous of

you." If there was any lingering doubt, Ewan was now convinced. He *had* completely misjudged Thea. She was nothing like he'd assumed at first.

She waved away both the tears and his praise. "It's the least I could do after coming here and making such a cake of myself by sneaking around and breaking my leg."

Ewan chuckled and stuck his hands in his coat pockets. "Oh, I wouldn't say that. Think of it this way, if you hadn't sneaked around and broken your leg, Phillip might not be speaking now."

Thea smiled and nodded. "That is a nice way to think of it. Thank you. I shall never regret having broken my leg then." She glanced over to where Phillip was standing, still speaking softly to the horse.

Thea sighed and rested her arms atop the stall door in front of her. She balanced herself and braced her wrapped leg against the ground. It felt good to stand, even if her leg hurt a bit.

Ewan took a step closer to her. He was less than a pace away from her. He towered above her. She turned to him and had to tilt her head back to look up into his face. Oh, why did the man have to be so handsome *and* smell so good? She didn't want to return his handkerchief. It smelled like him.

"In addition to Phillip's identity, I'm going to need you to keep one more secret, Thea," Ewan said softly, as he gazed into her eyes.

She swallowed the lump in her throat that had formed the moment he'd got so close to her. "What's that?" she asked in a whisper.

"That I did this." His mouth swooped down to capture hers.

# CHAPTER TWENTY-SIX

The moment Ewan's lips touched hers, Thea's mind raced. Her first thought, *what is he doing*, was quickly replaced by her second thought, *I hope he doesn't stop*.

At first the kiss was soft, inviting, and then he turned to place his body in front of hers, presumably so that Phillip wouldn't see if he turned around, and that's when the kiss became insistent, urging.

Ewan's tongue probed at her lips and she parted them. When she did, his mouth slanted across hers, shaping and molding, urging her to let her tongue play with his.

By the time he pulled his mouth away and stepped back one step, Thea was breathing heavily and shaking with desire. She'd been kissed before by some ham-handed would-be country suitors, but none of those missteps were anything like *this* kiss.

She stared up at Ewan with wide eyes as if he'd just done something to her she would never forget, because she was certain she wouldn't.

"I hope you'll forgive me for that," he said, clearing his throat, stepping back, and straightening his coat.

At a complete loss for words, all Thea could do was stare at him, her mouth opening and closing as if she was some sort of fish out of water, before Phillip's voice interrupted whatever she'd been intending to say.

"He's just as I remember him," Phillip called.

"He's been waiting for you," Ewan managed to call back as if he hadn't just kissed Thea so passionately she could barely remember her own name.

Thea continued to stare at him. How could he speak after that? How could he talk to Phillip as if nothing had even happened? Meanwhile, she was never going to be the same. She was thankful, however, that Ewan was so composed because one of them had to be.

Ewan stepped out from behind the stall and made his way to his friend to discuss the horse while Thea gaped after him. After all these days of wondering what it would be like, she'd finally been kissed by Lord Clayton...and she already wanted to kiss him again.

EWAN SPENT the next quarter of an hour telling Phillip the story of how he'd managed to buy not only his former horse, but all of his family's former possessions at the auction his distant cousin had held in London several weeks ago. Ewan was saving all of it for his friend. Words came out of Ewan's mouth and he managed to relate an entire cogent tale, but his mind was decidedly elsewhere. Namely on the kiss he'd just shared with Thea.

He shouldn't have done it. Of course he shouldn't have. He had no excuse for it, and it made little sense, but he simply couldn't help himself. After seeing the sincerity of her reaction to Phillip being reunited with the horse that she'd wanted for herself, he'd simply fallen a bit in love with the girl. That's all there was to it. Oh, he didn't necessarily believe in love, but he'd been wanting to kiss her for days and lately, he'd got the distinct impression that she wouldn't be unhappy if he did it. There had been only one way to find out and the emotions of the morning had got the best of him.

Only it wasn't just emotions. He was even now fighting a cockstand the likes of which he hadn't experienced in quite some time. He felt like an untried school lad, he was so unable to quiet down the rampaging demands of his body after the heat of her kiss. She hadn't just allowed him to kiss her, she'd kissed him back with all the passion he'd always known was in her.

The problem was...now he wanted her. And that was deuced inconvenient. She wasn't some widow or opera singer. She was an innocent young woman. A spinster perhaps, but the daughter of a peer, not someone he would trifle with and certainly not someone he could take to his bed. *Damn. Damn. Damn.* It *had* been a mistake to kiss her. How would he manage to live under the same roof with her for at least another fortnight if not longer? She'd been at his house for nearly three weeks now and Dr. Blanchard, who visited regularly, had indicated that it might be a total of six weeks before her leg could be moved enough to ride all the way home in a coach.

Ewan had walked away from her. He'd gone to talk to Phillip in order to give her time. He could tell she'd been dazed by the kiss. But he had no way of knowing if she wanted to slap him or kiss him again. He guessed it was the latter. She wasn't the type of woman who would be shy with a slap.

He needed to return to her. She had a broken leg and he'd left her propped against a stall door like a pitchfork. He turned to look at her. She was staring off into the distance of the stables. Her profile was lovely.

"Shall we go back?" he said to Phillip.

Phillip nodded, gave Alabaster one last pet, and the two men made their way to where Thea was standing. Before Ewan could move to help Thea into her wheelchair, she cleared her throat. "Phillip, would you be so kind as to help me sit?" she asked. "I'm certain Lord Clayton could use a break from me."

*On the contrary*, Ewan thought, stepping aside to allow Phillip to assist Thea back into her chair. The last thing he wanted was a break from her. In fact, he wanted more of her. Much more.

# CHAPTER TWENTY-SEVEN

The next day, Thea sat in her bed, her leg propped upon pillows, writing *another* letter to her brother. She had no idea why Anthony had chosen to abandon her, but she intended to send him a scathing reply. She'd already sent off a letter to her uncle in London days ago. In it, she'd briefly sketched out her circumstances— leaving out the bit about trying to break in Lord Clayton's stables while dressed as a lad—and asked Uncle Teddy to come fetch her immediately in order to save her reputation. If her uncle didn't reply, next she'd write to Lady Hophouse, her mother's closest friend.

*Someone* had to see the logic in Thea's argument and come for her. She had to get to get out of here. She'd already stayed far too long. Ewan had kissed her, and she had wanted it, and now she was having visions of marriage and children and oh, the whole thing was so complicated. One didn't marry someone whom one had met by sneaking around his house and breaking one's leg. It was preposterous.

She had an awful feeling that she was falling in love with Ewan. And that was something she could not allow to happen. Her mother had been quite clear on the subject when just before her accident, she'd told Thea the story of how she and Thea's father had met and married.

Mama had fallen madly in love with Father when she'd met him at a ball in London soon after her come out. She'd been convinced that Father loved her back, but Father had truly only been in love with her money and her family connections, both of which were quite impressive. They'd agreed to marry after only a few weeks of courting, which was quite normal. But it wasn't until weeks after the wedding that Mama realized that Father had a mistress in London. A mistress that he had no intention of relinquishing. He left Mama in the countryside and returned to his amusements in London as if he'd never taken a bride. He showed up long enough to impregnate his wife and produce his two offspring. Mama did her duty and gave birth, kept the estate, and presided as hostess whenever Father arrived from London with company. She also managed to convince him to have an annual Christmastide ball. It was the one time of year she could be certain he'd be home with her.

Thea's heart ached for her poor mother who had loved a man who never loved her back. She would never forget her mother's final words to her. "Never marry a man who doesn't love you back, Thea. It's pure torture." Those words had rung in her ears for the last six years.

In addition to being in mourning when it was time for her come-out, Thea had also been frightened of marriage. How, precisely, did one find a man who loved you back if men kept secrets like having mistresses stashed in London? The whole concept was horrifying. She'd managed to stay away from such subjects as love and marriage all these years and now Lord Clayton was making her wish for things she'd long ago abandoned. It was highly inconvenient, not to mention distressing. And she couldn't possibly think correctly about it while she was living under the same roof as the man. All she wanted to do was kiss him again. That wasn't helpful.

No, she had to get back home as quickly as possible, and if the only way to do that was to convince one of her relatives or friends to come and get her, so be it. She was on a letter-writing campaign. She turned her attention back to her brother's letter, re-reading it to ensure she'd made all her most important arguments.

Meanwhile, across the room, Maggie sat in a chair near the window, perusing the morning copy of the *Times*. Maggie loved to read the gossipy bits of the paper aloud. Thea listened with one ear. She was slightly amused by, but not particularly interested in, the *ton*'s gossip.

"Lady Haversham is hosting a musicale at her home in Berkeley Square," Maggie announced.

"What a pity I wasn't invited," Thea replied, her voice dripping with sarcasm.

"A musicale might do you good," Maggie retorted, without glancing up. "It's a much more appropriate pastime than sneaking into stables."

Thea arched a brow. "So *you* say."

Maggie ignored her and continued to the next bit of news.

Thea smiled to herself. She could just imagine the story that would appear in the paper the day it became known that the former Duke of Harlowe's brother hadn't died in the war after all and was taking his place in Society. Mag would fall off her chair. Of course Thea longed to tell her friend such important news, but she'd promised Ewan that she would keep it a secret and she would. As far as Maggie knew, Phillip was just a house guest and friend of Lord Clayton's.

"Apparently, Lady Cranberry's ball was a smash," Maggie said next. "Despite the fact that the ice sculpture melted precipitously and created a small flood near the dance floor, causing more than one dancer to slip."

"Did anyone break their leg?" Thea asked absently.

"If anyone did, it's not mentioned," Maggie replied with a sigh.

"Good, I wouldn't wish it on anyone," Thea replied, glaring at her own currently useless leg. "Though I'll soon have a wheelchair someone may borrow."

"Lord Whitmire and Miss Laura Footwinkle are to be married," Maggie reported next.

"Lord Whitmire is a blowhard," Thea replied. "And I've never heard of Miss Footwinkle."

"You should at least pretend to care about these things," Maggie said with a note of scolding in her voice. The maid shook her head.

"Why should I, Mag, when I have *you* to care for it all for me?" Thea replied with a wide smile. "But if it makes you feel any better, I wish Miss Footwinkle luck. She'll need it if she has to listen to Lord Whitmire's dull stories the remainder of her life."

Shaking her head, the maid made a few more random announcements that Thea barely paid attention to, until a small, short gasp came from Maggie's throat.

Thea glanced up. Her friend's face had turned a ghastly shade of white. A skitter of apprehension traced its way down Thea's spine. "What is it, Maggie?"

Maggie lifted her gaze from the paper and met Thea's stare. Maggie's dark eyes were filled with trepidation.

"You're frightening me," Thea said warily. "Tell me. What is it?"

"I'm afraid you won't like this," Maggie replied with an obvious gulp.

"What?" Thea heard the note of rising panic in her own voice. "Bring me the paper, please."

Maggie slowly rose from her seat and walked even more slowly toward the bed. When she finally got there, she handed the paper to Thea, opened to the spot she'd been reading. She pointed to some wording near the middle of the page.

Thea's eyes scanned the area until they alighted on what Maggie had obviously been horrified by.

*This author has it from an impeccable authority that under the utmost secrecy, in Devon, Lady Theodora Ballard, daughter of the Earl of Blackstone, has been living under the same roof as Viscount Clayton!*

# CHAPTER TWENTY-EIGHT

"**B**loody hell," Ewan called out as he scanned the *Times* gossip page. "Humbolt, get in here."

Humbolt materialized at the door to Ewan's study moments later. "Yes, my lord."

"Call for Dr. Blanchard. Tell him he must come immediately. Then send a letter to Lord Blackstone. Tell him the same."

"Yes, my lord." Humbolt nodded and hurried away to do what he'd been asked.

Ewan cursed again under his breath. He was accustomed to reading the gossip rags because gossip—innocuous as it may seem—often proved useful when negotiating with certain gentlemen in Parliament. One never knew when a bit of information might prove useful in convincing a peer to listen to reason. An informed member of Parliament was a powerful member of Parliament, or so Ewan liked to think.

He prided himself, however, on keeping his *own* name out of the papers for anything other than his work in Parliament. Gossip was not something associated with him. For good reason.

*Until now.* He cursed a third time.

DR. BLANCHARD ARRIVED FIRST. He was summoned directly to Ewan's study where Ewan was pacing the floor, his options looking bleaker and bleaker.

"Have you seen the paper this morning?" he asked the doctor.

Dr. Blanchard shifted uncomfortably on his feet and cleared his throat. "I have, my lord."

"Then you know why I've summoned you so quickly."

The doctor nodded.

"We must know what our options are," Ewan continued. "Lady Theodora has been here for three weeks. How is her leg? Can she be moved? Has the bone healed enough?"

"I will need to examine her again, of course, my lord. It certainly will be better to move her now than it would have been three weeks ago, but there remains a risk."

Ewan bit the inside of his cheek and nodded. "Very well. Lord Blackstone will be here shortly. We'll discuss the options with him. I fear we have few."

"WHAT HAVE YOU LEARNED?" Thea asked Maggie as soon as the maid came rushing back into Thea's bedchamber.

Thea had sent Maggie on a mission to discover what she could about Lord Clayton's whereabouts and whether he'd learned of the story in the *Times*. It made her exceedingly nervous that no one had mentioned anything to her yet.

"Your father is here," Maggie reported, wringing her hands. "He just arrived. Mr. Humbolt is showing him to Lord Clayton's study right now."

Thea pedaled her wheelchair toward the door. If she'd ever wished there was a time she could stand up and pace, it was now. "Father? Here? Why, that must be because they plan to discuss the entire affair."

"It looks that way," Maggie agreed.

Thea pressed her lips together tightly. "Lord Clayton hasn't sent for me, which means they plan to discuss it without me. That's unconscionable."

"Perhaps they don't want to worry you, Thea," Maggie offered.

"Worry me? First of all, I'm already quite worried. Secondly, it's *my* life. *My* future. *My* family. *My* scandal! They cannot possibly believe they should be discussing the fallout without me present."

Thea pedaled up to the door and stopped. "Open the door, please, Maggie, and call for the footmen to carry me downstairs. I refuse to allow those blasted men to meet without me."

MINUTES LATER, Thea and her chair were downstairs and being pushed by Giles directly toward Ewan's study. Maggie hadn't argued with Thea's decision to interrupt the gentlemen's meeting. Even Maggie knew not to argue with Thea when she was as determined as she was at the moment. Instead of trying to dissuade her, Maggie had opened the door immediately and rang for James and Giles who both hurried up to assist.

As Thea and Giles approached the study door, she motioned for the footman to be silent and then dismissed him. She pedaled herself the two or three lengths left to put her ear to the study door.

"I'm sorry this happened," came her father's voice.

Thea rolled his eyes. How sorry was he? The man had left her here, knowing full well a scandal would ensue if anyone were to tell, and someone obviously had.

"No, I am the one who owes you an apology, my lord," came Ewan's reply. "It would seem someone in my staff provided the information to the papers."

"You cannot know that for certain, Clayton," came Father's reply. "Two of my servants are aware of Thea's being here. It may well have been one of them."

Thea narrowed her eyes. How dare Father accuse Maggie of spreading the rumor? Thea doubted it was Giles either. The obvious culprit was loose-lipped Rosalie, though Thea supposed they would never be able to prove it.

"At this point it no longer matters who told. The damage has been done," came Ewan's voice next. There was a long pause before he continued. "I suppose we'd both agree there is only one way to handle this situation."

Thea held her breath. His voice sounded decidedly resigned.

"I know what you have in mind, Clayton," Father replied. "And I quite agree."

*What? What did he have in mind?* Thea's heart was pounding so rapidly in her ears she had to strain to hear.

"I'll summon my solicitor," Ewan said sharply. "We'll draw up a marriage contract."

Thea gasped.

"If it's any consolation, Clayton, she has a large and apt dowry," Father replied.

"I'm not worried about a dowry," came Ewan's reply. "I'm much more worried about how I shall explain this to my *fiancée*."

Heat and cold suffused Thea's body simultaneously. She was melting. She was freezing. The walls of the corridor were closing around her. No. This couldn't be happening.

This could *not* be happening. She braced a hand on the wall next to the door to steady herself. She was going to be ill.

*Fiancée? Fiancée!* What? Thea had had no idea that Ewan had a *fiancée!* No, no. This couldn't be happening. It wouldn't be happening! Not if she had any say in the matter. And she *would* have a say in the matter. There was no possible way she was going to marry a man who didn't want her. Who was marrying her out of a sense of obligation over a mistake that *she'd* caused in the first place. She would not be a burden to Ewan the rest of her life.

*If it's any consolation, Clayton…* Her father's words echoed through her brain in a maddening loop. But worse were Ewan's words in reply. *I'm much more worried about how I shall explain this to my* fiancée. The man had kissed her, yet he had a *fiancée*. He was a rogue. A scoundrel. A cheat.

Thea didn't remember how she made it back to the staircase and managed to call for the footmen again. But once she was in her bedchamber again, she quickly shut the door behind her and wheeled around to face Maggie.

"Pack my trunk immediately, please," she said, barely able to breathe. "We're going home with Father."

# CHAPTER TWENTY-NINE

**E**wan was barely paying attention to the details of the contract that was being drawn up. He'd summoned his solicitor immediately after he and Lord Blackstone had decided that a marriage had to take place. The solicitor was currently ensconced in Ewan's study, composing the marriage contract between Ewan and Thea.

It was quite unlike Ewan to disregard the details. Normally, he paid attention to every word of such a document. A marriage contract was something he'd be tied to for the rest of his life. There were huge implications to this contract, but he couldn't summon the will to care about the details. All he could think about was how much his life had changed in the few short weeks since meeting Lady Theodora Ballard.

Only a matter of days ago, he'd been leading a perfectly ordered life. One in which he knew precisely what he'd be doing from each day to the next because he'd bloody well planned it. But ever since Thea had arrived on his doorstep, there had been one catastrophe after another ending in a marriage contract being drawn. How in the world had this happened?

The solicitor continued asking a series of questions and Ewan answered with monosyllabic replies as he envisioned himself informing Lord Malcolm, Lydia's father, that there would no longer be an understanding between himself and his daughter. Lord Malcolm wouldn't be pleased, but he would be reasonable. Ewan had assumed for so long that he'd marry Lydia, he couldn't wrap his mind around the thought that that would no longer be true. He'd had no intention of getting married anytime *soon*, of course, and perhaps that said something about his eagerness to marry Lydia, or lack thereof, to be more precise.

But when he thought of marrying Thea, he found himself…looking forward to it. Certainly looking forward to the wedding night. It was surprising, to say the least, but there it was, a sense of…anticipation in his belly.

Marriages in their set were based on sound principles such as two families uniting to form a more powerful one. That's why he'd wanted to marry Lydia. He hadn't thought much past it other than that. Lydia seemed an agreeable enough girl. She was born and bred in a decent household. She should make a fine wife. That was all there was to it. Now, he was faced with the prospect of marrying for an altogether different reason…to prevent a scandal. And while marrying for politics might not be the best reason to marry, marrying to prevent a scandal certainly had to be among the worst.

Ewan stared out the window of his study, not even seeing the meadow beyond. He may not have asked for any of this, may not have expected it, but he had to do the honorable thing and marry Thea. He had no choice. It was the only action that would save her reputation now that the gossip rags had got ahold of the news that she'd been living under his roof. Even properly chaperoned. It didn't matter. The sordid implication was there in black and white for the entire *ton* to read.

As the solicitor called out item after item that needed to be decided upon, Ewan heard himself agreeing to whatever Lord Blackstone wanted. The dowry was substantial. He had no objections. Thea would be allowed to retain control over money left to her from her mother. He had no objections. Thea would use a portion of her dowry for a *trousseau*. Standard fare.

"There are certain things you should know that Thea will insist upon," Lord Blackstone announced.

Ewan arched a brow. "Such as?"

"She'll want to ride whenever she chooses," Blackstone replied.

Ewan's snort of laughter filled the room. "I'd like to see anyone try to keep her from it."

Blackstone arched a brow. "I'm afraid you're going to have your hands full, Clayton."

Ewan eyed the older man carefully. If Thea had been *his* daughter, instead of acting as if she'd be a burden to the man she was to marry, he'd be doing whatever he could to tout her virtues. The young woman Ewan had come to know over the last few weeks was witty, wise, and beautiful. She knew precisely what she wanted, and she brooked no foolishness. She was a daughter Blackstone should be proud of. Ewan shook his head. Blackstone didn't deserve his daughter. At the moment, Ewan wasn't certain he deserved her either.

OVER AN HOUR LATER, the contract had been completed. The solicitor pushed the document in front of Ewan and handed him a quill. Ewan stared at the paper and then glanced up at

Blackstone. "I think we should ask Thea before we sign it. To ensure she's amenable to the plan."

Blackstone narrowed his eyes, confusion obvious in their depths. "Ask Theodora?"

Ewan had to bite the inside of his cheek to refrain from pointing out to the man that his daughter preferred to be called Thea.

"Yes, what if she objects?" Ewan asked.

"She doesn't have a choice," Blackstone replied curtly.

Ewan arched a brow. "Is that how you see it?"

The earl wouldn't meet his eyes. "Leave it to me to inform Theodora."

# CHAPTER THIRTY

"We've come to a decision," Father pronounced as he strode through Thea's bedchamber door at Clayton's house.

Thea was imminently prepared for such a pronouncement. "So have I. I'm going home with you immediately." She motioned to the packed trunks, her large one and Maggie's small one that sat next to the door.

Father narrowed his eyes. "You must listen to me, Theodora. We've made the best decision for your future."

Thea sat up straight and raised her voice. "Let me make myself clear. I am *not* staying here. Whatever plans you've made for me you can explain to me *at home*. I refuse to remain here as the subject of gossip from some unknown monger. I don't care if my leg falls *off*."

Her father clenched his jaw and anger flashed in his gray eyes. But he clearly understood how very serious she was. "Fine. I'll take you home. But we shall discuss your future on the way."

Thea didn't care. She'd won the first battle, which was to get out of Lord Clayton's house immediately. Given the fact that she had no idea who was spreading the gossip about her, leaving was the first and most important thing to do. She had no intention of marrying Clayton and staying here a moment longer would only serve to make that decision more difficult to justify. Now that the news had hit the papers, no doubt the neighbors would all come to see for themselves. For all she knew, there were already some on the way.

~

NOT AN HOUR LATER, Thea, Maggie, and all of their *accoutrements* were loaded into Lord Blackstone's coach. Giles and James had put the wheelchair inside of a wagon that would travel back separately.

Thea had even managed to convince her father that they shouldn't be seen in the foyer taking leave of their host. Instead, she promised to write Clayton a thank you letter when she was settled back at home. For now, she sent her thanks to the viscount by way of her father, who returned to the study to let Clayton know that he'd be taking his daughter home immediately.

Inside the coach, they did their best to accommodate Thea's leg, propping it on a set of pillows and blankets. But as the conveyance traveled along the rutted country roads, the occasional bump was upsetting enough to cause Thea to cry out in pain. She gritted her teeth and tried to keep in any grunts or groans, but every once in a while, she couldn't help herself.

Several times her father tried to broach the subject of the ridiculous engagement. At some point, Thea realized that playing up the pain in her leg kept her father from attempting to discuss it.

Meanwhile, Maggie sat tensely at Thea's side, attempting

to concentrate on her needlework and wincing every time Thea cried out.

"Theodora, we must discuss your future," Father finally demanded when they were less than a quarter hour from Blackstone Hall. "Lord Clayton and I have—"

"Gah!" Thea cried before putting the back of her hand to her forehead for maximum dramatic effect. "My leg is throbbing and I'm exhausted. Can we not speak of it tomorrow after I've had a chance to rest, Father?"

"We must have a care for your reputation," Father snapped back.

Thea clenched her jaw. "Yes, we *should* have had that care when you forced me to remain at Lord Clayton's house after my accident."

That was enough to silence her father for the remainder of the ride home. Thank heavens. Thea stared out the window. The day was gray and cold, just like her thoughts. She watched as the coach passed the leafless trees, their black branches outlined against the chilly gray skies as thoughts of her time with Clayton flashed through her mind.

She did regret not having a chance to say good-bye to Phillip. He was such a nice man. Sweet and kind and thoughtful. Nowhere near as maddening as Clayton had been when she first met him. She would write Phillip to say good-bye. She would encourage him to see Alabaster as often as possible.

Alabaster. Would she ever be able to see the horse again? If she were to visit, the gossip might make its way to the papers. *Blast.* She closed her eyes. She would have to worry about that later. She was far too exhausted to worry about it at the moment.

But Thea couldn't sleep. The pain from the ride bouncing her broken leg had her clenching her jaw, and if that wasn't uncomfortable enough, each time she tried to rest, one horrible, confusing, surprising thought kept torturing her: Clayton had a *fiancée*.

A *fiancée*. The man had been betrothed the entire time she'd been at his home and he'd never mentioned it. What sort of a scoundrel was he? He'd *kissed* her for heaven's sake. He was the worst kind of cad.

He was exactly who her mother had warned her against.

Thea tried to picture Clayton's betrothed. He hadn't mentioned a name. Had she ever met the young lady? Was she Thea's age? No doubt she was younger. She might even be a debutante. Eighteen years old. Had she just made her debut last spring? Did she have long straight blond hair and sparkling blue eyes like many of the most popular debutantes did? Did she do things like play the pianoforte and sing like a lark? No doubt she wasn't ill-tempered and stubborn like Thea was. No doubt she wasn't the type of young lady who would dress as a lad and sneak into Clayton's stables in the middle of the night. And she probably wasn't the type who would break her leg while doing it.

Oh, what did it matter? Thea would not—*would not*—marry Lord Clayton. They couldn't force her to do it. They wouldn't dare. Which meant soon Clayton would be free to marry the young lady of his choosing. She of the long blond hair and larklike voice. Thea wouldn't spend another moment wondering about her identity. It was nothing but a waste of time. She had much more important things to think about, like how in the world would she convince her father that she would *not*, under any circumstances, agree to marry Lord Clayton. It was certain to be the biggest row they'd ever had, but she was determined to win at all costs.

# CHAPTER THIRTY-ONE

E wan watched from the shadow of the stable wall as
Alabaster jumped the low fence with Phillip upon
his back. Forrester had been working with Phillip
and Alabaster every afternoon for days now. According to
Forrester, Phillip was improving at a record pace.

Phillip smiled and waved at Ewan. Ewan returned the
gesture. It was amazing, the progress Phillip had made in the
days since Ewan had introduced him to Thea. And there was
no doubting it was Thea's influence that had helped his
friend so much. She'd spent hours speaking to him quietly.
They'd discussed Alabaster a great deal. Thea had told him
stories about the horse's foal-hood. Ewan had heard Phillip
chuckling and replying with stories of his own.

There was no denying it. In the few weeks Thea had been
there, Phillip had made more progress than in all the months
Ewan had been desperately trying to help him. It was
nothing short of an amazing transformation.

Thea. Where was she right now? Ewan leaned back
against the stable wall, closed his eyes, and expelled his
breath. All he knew was that she was no longer at Clayton

Manor. He should have signed the contract. If he had, there would be little Thea could do to refuse the marriage. But Ewan didn't want her to come to him as a wife by force. Thea was beyond stubborn. If she set her mind against the marriage, even though it was obviously the only reasonable thing to do, she would never agree to it.

Asking her first was the right thing to do, of course. Ewan had even planned to drop to one knee and do the thing properly, but Blackstone had informed him that Thea was concerned with additional gossip and wanted to go home immediately. Apparently, she didn't care about the damage that could be done to her leg. She hadn't even given Ewan a chance to say good-bye. Those things already boded ill. Add to that the fact that she and her father were always at sixes and sevens and Ewan held little hope that she would readily agree to a marriage.

Ewan intended to pay Thea a visit after she had a chance to recover from her no doubt painful journey home. He hoped her leg hadn't been too affected by the ride. He wanted to see her, he realized. To talk to her again.

Ewan pushed himself away from the stable wall and began walking back toward the house, leaving Forrester with Phillip. Ewan needed to prepare himself and his household for a viscountess. It was something he hadn't planned on so soon in life, but it was happening just the same. Though admittedly with a different bride than the one he'd originally expected.

Lord Blackstone wasn't particularly well-connected politically and a marriage with Thea clearly wouldn't be as advantageous for Ewan's career as it would have been if he'd married Lady Lydia. But Ewan had no regrets. There was little chance he'd ever become bored with Thea as his wife, she loved horses as much or more than he did and kissing her made his blood sing. She was also quite special. He'd learned that about her in their weeks together. Lady Theodora Ballard was one of a kind.

Ewan could only hope her father didn't bungle the announcement so profoundly that she set her cap against marrying him entirely. Because once that happened, there was little chance she'd ever change her mind.

# CHAPTER THIRTY-TWO

A slight knock on her bedchamber door made Thea cringe. It was her father. They'd been home for over a day now and she'd exhausted her pleas of being tired and in pain in order to keep her father away. Very well. She'd put off the conversation long enough. The time had come. She sucked in a deep breath, pushed herself up on the pillows, and straightened her shoulders. She had to be prepared. "Come in," she finally called, folding her hands in front of her.

The door opened and her father strode inside and bowed to her. "I trust you're feeling better this morning."

"Less tired at least," she allowed, inclining her head to the side.

Her father grabbed his lapels and cleared his throat. "We must speak about your future, Theodora."

She tried to keep her voice pleasant and calm. "I am well aware of what you plan for my future, Father, but I must tell you I disagree."

"Disagree with what?" Her father narrowed his eyes on her.

She folded her arms across her chest. "With your plan to marry me off to Lord Clayton."

"Theodora, you must understand—"

"I understand perfectly." Her words came out in a clipped tone. So much for calm and pleasant. "The two of you discussed it, without my input, and decided quite high-handedly that a wedding would be the best way to handle the fallout and the potential scandal of my having stayed at Lord Clayton's house for so long. I don't agree with you."

Father's jaw clenched and his lips turned into a thin line. "At the risk of angering you further, Theodora, I don't require your agreement."

Her eyes flashed fire and she clenched her fists into the covers. This man may have been able to coerce her beautiful, sweet, quiet mother, but Thea was not about to let him frighten *her* into an unwanted marriage. The rest of her life, her future happiness depended on it. She would not die a wasting death in her bedchamber while her husband was in London with his mistress as her mother had. "On the contrary," she shot back, "you do need my agreement. If you plan a wedding, I promise you I will not be there on the appointed day."

"What do you mean?" Father narrowed his eyes on her.

"I mean exactly what I said. You cannot have a wedding without a bride. No matter what I have to do, I will not be there."

"Are you threatening to harm yourself?" Father demanded.

She shrugged. That just showed how little her father knew her. She would not harm herself. She hadn't even considered that thought, but if he wanted to believe that was a possibility, so be it. It suited her purposes to allow him to think that she had more than one option. "Or run away," she replied, giving him a tight smile.

"Run away? Where would you go?" Father clipped.

She'd never wished she could stand more than this moment. "I'm hardly going to tell you that, but rest assured the scandal that would result from Lord Clayton being left at the altar would be much larger than my ruined reputation over the gossip in the paper."

Her father's voice raised to nearly a shout. "May I remind you, Theodora, that this scandal and everything about it is *your* fault to begin with?"

Her words shot like bullets through clenched teeth. "May I remind you, Father, that I asked you to take me home after I broke my leg and you refused?"

Her father cursed under his breath. "You are stubborn to your own detriment, Theodora. Can you not see this is the best choice for your future?"

"Can you not see that I am the best judge of what is best for my future? I do not wish to marry Lord Clayton."

"What does that have to do with it? You'll be saving yourself from additional gossip. You'll be sparing your brother and me, as well."

"Spare me the recriminations, Father. The fact remains I refuse to allow the two of you to decide my future so cavalierly."

Her father turned sharply toward the door. "So be it, Theodora. You may remain an unwanted spinster the rest of your life."

# CHAPTER THIRTY-THREE

Ewan slammed his palm against the top of his desk in his study, making the papers along with the quill and ink well bounce. "Damn it!"

Humbolt came rushing to the door. "Is something wrong, my lord? May I assist you with anything?"

"Yes, something is bloody well wrong, but no, it's nothing you can assist with," Ewan replied. "My apologies for startling you, Humbolt."

Humbolt bowed and took his leave while Ewan picked up the letter from Blackstone that he'd just read and scanned it again. It was every bit as maddening reading it the second time.

*Clayton,*

*I regret to inform you that Theodora refuses to agree to the marriage. I told her to prepare to marry you but she will not obey. She's even threatened to run off if I force the matter. I'm afraid if insist, she'll harm herself. I apologize for all of the trouble my daughter has caused you of late. This is now my family's shame to bear and we shall involve you no further in our problems.*

*Theodora has made her decision. She shall be forced to suffer the consequences.*

Ewan clenched his jaw. That fool. Blackstone *had* bungled it. Just as Ewan feared he would. You couldn't *tell* Thea anything. You had to *ask* her. Learn her thoughts on the matter. *Discuss* it with her. And that's precisely what Ewan had intended to do. Only now he seriously wondered if Thea would even accept his call if he were to visit. *Damn. Damn. Damn.* This whole affair had turned into a mess.

Along with the letter from Blackstone, which Ewan had chosen to read first for some reason, was a letter from Thea. He ripped it open and scanned the page, already disappointed at the short length of the missive.

*Lord Clayton,*

*Words cannot express the depth of gratitude I have for your extreme kindness. My deepest apologies for the trouble I have caused. Please give Alabaster an apple for me.*

*Lady Theodora Ballard*

That was it? Those were the only words he was to receive from her? She knew that he and her father had drawn up a marriage contract. She intended to act as if that hadn't even happened? All three of them knew if the men insisted and signed the thing, she would have no choice but to marry him. But Ewan didn't want that, and her father apparently didn't either. Blackstone had even mentioned that she might harm herself. Ewan seriously doubted that. He would, however, believe that she'd run away if it came down to it and that would cause an even larger scandal. He could just picture the gossip rags getting hold of the story that the two had become engaged and Lady Theodora had fled in order to escape the marriage. No. That would never do.

If they didn't marry, Theodora's reputation along with that of her father and brother would be tarnished, but eventually, the *ton* would move on to the next scandal. And as long as Thea didn't intend to marry (and by all accounts she obviously didn't) she'd just fade into the lore of spinsters with hints of scandal in their past. It might not be fair or right, but Ewan could continue with his life and his plans relatively unscathed.

He needed to face the fact that Thea clearly wanted nothing to do with him. So much so that she preferred the life of a spinster, potential scandal, and would even run away *from her own home*, in order to keep from having to marry him.

Ewan scrubbed his hands through his hair. Damn it. Fine then. He'd attempted to do the gentlemanly thing. He'd tried to be honorable and offer Thea the protection of his name. If she didn't want it, refused it outright, threatened to flee from it even, he had no further obligation to the young lady. She'd been the one who'd sneaked into his stables. She'd been the one who'd fallen and broken her leg. She'd been the one who'd become an unwanted houseguest. And now she was the one who was refusing his help. So be it. He would go on with his life and forget about Lady Theodora Ballard and the complete chaos she'd caused in his affairs for several weeks this autumn. He would return to his normally ordered, carefully planned life.

# CHAPTER THIRTY-FOUR

Thea wheeled herself around to stare out the window of the drawing room. She'd just finished writing a letter to Phillip to say good-bye. She hadn't seen her father in the two days since they'd argued. The barbs she'd traded with him seemed to play on a never-ending loop through her mind. *So be it, Theodora. You may remain an unwanted spinster the rest of your life.*

Her father was right. She was unwanted. But she hadn't been able to bring herself to tell him that *that* was the real reason for her refusal to marry Lord Clayton. Her father already believed she was a spoiled, selfish spinster. Why should she go to any trouble to disabuse him of that notion? Besides, even if she had told him that she knew Lord Clayton wanted another woman, her father would merely brush off her concerns as unimportant. Father was much more interested in the fact that Clayton *would* marry her versus caring that the man didn't *want* to marry her. She was about to have what she feared would be a very similar argument with her brother.

Anthony entered the drawing room behind Thea. He'd just returned from a trip to London, and she had quite a few things to say to him. It was freezing outside and despite the blanket on her lap, she shivered. She should move her wheelchair closer to the fireplace, but she couldn't seem to muster the energy.

"How are you feeling? How is your leg?" Anthony asked after shutting the door behind him and moving toward the settee in the center of the room.

"It's healing," she answered curtly.

"Father tells me that Dr. Blanchard was here and he said your leg should heal properly despite the coach ride."

"Yes. I'm quite fortunate." Thea was done with small talk. She wheeled herself around to face her brother head-on. "Why didn't you come for me? Why didn't you write back?"

Anthony sighed and scrubbed his hand through his hair. "I'm sorry, Thea. I truly am. But I spoke to Father about it at length and he insisted that you remain there. And I did write back."

Thea clutched at the arms of her chair. "Since when do you listen to Father? And you only wrote back once to say you weren't coming and that took long enough."

Anthony braced his hands atop the back of the settee, clutching the fabric. "I couldn't very well sneak you home without Father knowing about it. What would you have me do, hide you in the cellar?"

Thea's sighed was filled with frustration. She wheeled herself closer to her brother. "I don't understand why Father was so set on my staying there. He knew the risk to my reputation, the risk to our family."

"I did mention it, more than once," Anthony replied, lifting one brow. "It seems he was more worried about your leg healing properly than our family name."

Thea narrowed her eyes. "Why do I doubt that?"

"Be that as it may," Anthony replied. "I'm sorry I didn't come for you. I'm sorry I didn't stand up to Father."

"No," Thea replied with another sigh. She lowered her chin to her chest and stared blankly into her lap. "I'm the one who should be sorry. I'm the one who went to Lord Clayton's estate and broke my leg. I'm to blame entirely. I owe you an apology for ruining your prospects."

Anthony came over and squatted next to her chair. "Don't worry about me, Thea. You know how the *ton* works as well as I do. I am an unmarried future earl. Men are always more protected than women in these situations. I'm worried about *your* reputation, *your* future."

Thea folded her hands atop the blanket. "The time for worrying about my reputation has come and gone. I've long since become a spinster. I would hate for this gossip to affect your future prospects."

Anthony squeezed her cold hand. "By the time I am ready to take a wife, no one will even remember this nonsense." Her brother stood and stepped toward the fireplace, leaning an arm against the mantel, he faced her. "Now, as for you being a spinster…Father told me you've refused Clayton's offer of marriage."

"Of course I did," Thea shot back.

Her brother folded his arms over his chest and eyed her down the length of his nose. "May I ask why?"

Thea shook her head impatiently. "I should think it would be obvious why. I have no intention of ruining that man's life."

Anthony's brows shot up. "Ruining his life?"

"Yes. Marrying him would be forcing him into an unwanted marriage with a woman who inserted herself into his life in the first place. Lord Clayton has been nothing but kind to me. I owe him an apology, not an unwanted future with an unwanted wife."

Her brother gave her a dubious look. "From what I know about Clayton, he's not the sort to be forced into doing anything."

Thea gave her brother an impatient glare. "What would you call it, then? He obviously only offered for me to do the honorable thing."

"He *is* honorable," Anthony agreed, "but that's not a bad thing, Thea. You're the daughter of an earl. It's not as if Clayton would be marrying beneath him."

Thea dropped her gaze to her lap. "He's engaged to someone else."

"Are you certain? I'd never read about that in any of the papers." She could hear the skepticism in Anthony's voice.

"I heard it from his own lips," Thea replied. She lifted her head to see her brother's reaction.

"Well." Anthony's mouth snapped shut. He rubbed his chin, still looking a bit skeptical. "I suppose that does change things somewhat. But I'm certain Clayton wouldn't have agreed to it if he hadn't been willing to marry you."

Thea fought the tears that stung the backs of her eyes. "There is a large difference between *wanting* to marry and *agreeing* to marry," she said softly.

Anthony's voice grew softer too. "Do you *want* to be a spinster, Thea? Don't you want your own home? Your own family?"

The tears threatened to spill. Thea swung her chair around to face the windows again. "I'll tell you what I don't want. I don't want to force a man to marry me."

Anthony cursed under his breath. "Damn it, Thea. Why must you be so stubborn? I truly believe you're making a mistake."

Thea stared out the window at the gray skies. *Never marry a man who doesn't love you back, Thea. It's pure torture.*

"No," Thea replied in a whisper, wrapping her arms around herself and shivering from the cold. "If I married Lord Clayton, *that* would be the biggest mistake of my life."

## CHAPTER THIRTY-FIVE

Beau Bellham, the Marquess of Bellingham, had been at Ewan's house for two days. Ewan had summoned his good friend there by writing him a letter. They needed to discuss Phillip's future. And Beau, a spy for the Home Office as well as a marquess, was the perfect person to discuss such matters. Ewan, Bell, and Phillip were sitting in the study in the late afternoon discussing that exact subject. Ewan and Phillip were enjoying a glass of brandy, while Bell, who famously didn't drink alcohol, was having a glass of water.

Ewan had begun the same sentence twice and both times he'd let it trail off as he stared past his friends out the windows of the study. For some reason, Ewan was imagining Thea riding Alabaster through the meadow, laughing and tossing her long dark hair.

There had been no laughter in the house since Thea had gone. There had been no life. He and Phillip had begun speaking to each other in monosyllabic words. The things Ewan had done for pleasure before Thea had resided under his roof were no longer particularly pleasurable. None of it made any sense. He'd been perfectly content to take his meals alone before Thea had arrived, but now when Humbolt served him, he sorely felt the absence of her presence at the end of the table, laughing and jesting and answering his questions and asking her own. Phillip had replaced her at the dinner table of late but even his old friend's company couldn't make up for Thea's loss.

She'd been unpredictable and unconventional. Both things that Ewan would have sworn weeks ago were undesirable to him, but now when he stared at the empty spot at the dining room table where she should have been, all he felt was the loss of her presence. He'd come to rely on their talks, her company.

The truth was, he'd written Bell to get a little more company. This time of year, Ewan normally returned to London to see his mother, visit friends, and participate in a variety of holiday parties to which he was invited.

This year, he told himself he was staying away due to the scandal in the papers. He would allow time for the commotion to die down before he returned to the city. But deep down, he truly hoped Thea would change her mind and agree to the marriage contract. He'd stayed in the country, day after day, waiting on tenterhooks for another letter from Lord Blackstone telling him that Thea had reconsidered. It made no sense, and he couldn't even explain why he hoped for such a letter, but he did. And he was a bloody fool because no such letter appeared to be forthcoming. It had been nearly a fortnight.

"What were you about to say?" Bell asked from the other side of the desk.

"I— What?" Ewan blinked and refocused his gaze on the marquess.

"You were saying something about how we should escort Phillip back to London when the time comes," Bell said, eyeing Ewan warily from his seat in the large leather chair in front of Ewan's desk.

Phillip glanced up from his brandy glass. "Don't be too harsh on him, Bell. The man is missing his houseguest."

Bell frowned. "What do you mean? You're right here."

"Not me," Phillip said, the hint of a smile playing about his lips. "His *other* houseguest."

Bell turned his full attention to Ewan. "Other houseguest? What am I missing?"

Ewan glared at Phillip. "Thank you for mentioning it, *Your Grace*."

Phillip inclined his head. His smile had widened. "You're quite welcome."

Ewan expelled a breath before facing Bell's questioning stare. "Don't you read the papers, Bell?"

"Papers?" Bell frowned again.

"Specifically, the *Times*," Ewan ventured.

"The gossip pages of the *Times* to be precise," Phillip added.

Bell rolled his eyes. "No. I'm somewhat busy doing His Majesty's bidding during a time of war, I'm not exactly interested in the *ton*'s silly gossip."

Ewan brought his brandy glass to his lips, but before taking a sip, he said, "I had a houseguest for a few weeks this autumn. A lady. Lady Theodora Ballard."

Bell shook his head. "I'm not familiar with the name."

"She's young. Early twenties. Lives here in Devon," Ewan replied, a vision of Thea's beautiful face haunting his memories. "She's the daughter of the Earl of Blackstone."

Bell's brow furrowed. "What was she doing staying here if she lives in Devon?"

"She, er, broke her leg here," Ewan said, before clearing his throat.

Bell eyed him warily. "Broke her leg?"

Ewan set his glass on the desktop in front of him and threaded his fingers together. "It's a long story and the details aren't important, but Dr. Blanchard said she shouldn't be moved so she stayed here for a bit."

"A bit?" Bell arched a brow.

"A few weeks," Ewan clarified.

"Lovely young lady, simply lovely," Phillip added, taking a sip from his glass.

"But what does that have to do with the gossip pages of the *Times*?" Bell asked.

"Oh, right. Well, the *Times* somehow got wind of the fact that Lady Theodora was staying here and published the rumor."

"Somehow got wind?" Bell arched a brow.

"Yes, we've yet to discover how that happened, but that's not the point. The point is that I offered for Lady Thea, but I'm supposed to become engaged to Lady Lydia Malcolm one day."

Both of Bell's brows shot up. "What? That's the first I've heard of that."

Ewan shrugged. "Nothing official. Just some preliminary discussion with her father. It was to be—ahem, *is* to be— a politically advantageous marriage."

"All right," Bell said. "But what does that have to do with Lady Theodora?"

"Lady Thea showed up and broke her leg," Phillip said, taking yet another sip of brandy.

Bell swiveled his head back and forth between the two men. "Wait. Clayton, are you *marrying* Lady Thea?"

"Not any longer," Ewan said simply, picking up his glass once more.

"What? Why?" Bell looked completely confused.

"Suffice it to say the lady prefers to live down the scandal rather than to marry me," Ewan replied with a sigh.

"And Clayton here has been moping about it since she left," Phillip interjected.

Ewan drew his brows together in a sharp frown. "I do not mope."

"Oh? Pardon me. I must have mistaken your silence and unhappiness for moping," Phillip replied with a laugh.

Ewan groaned and rubbed his face with both hands. "Oh, God. Have I been moping?"

"Don't be too hard on yourself, old chap. I do believe you miss her," Phillip said. "I miss her too."

"Do you miss Lydia?" Bell asked, his eyes narrowed on Ewan.

Ewan thought about the question for a moment before slowly shaking his head. "I've never missed Lydia. I barely know her."

"But you do miss Thea?" Bell wanted to know.

Ewan rubbed his face again. He rested his bended arm atop his head and leaned back in his chair. "If I'm being honest...yes."

Bell pursed his lips and finally took a sip from his own glass. "Well, well, well. Sounds to me as if someone may have fallen in love."

Ewan nearly spit the drink he'd just taken. "Love! Absolutely not, I simply—"

"Miss her company and think of her constantly?" Phillip supplied helpfully, raising his glass as if in a toast.

"I never said I think of her constantly," Ewan shot back, frowning fiercely at his friend.

"But you do, don't you?" Phillip blinked at him and gave him a wholly innocent smile.

Ewan sat silently stewing for a few moments. How the hell did Phillip know that he thought of Thea constantly? Was it that obvious? Was it written on his face? "It doesn't matter," Ewan replied, tossing a hand in the air. "She's refused me and that's the end to it."

"How do you know she's not pining for you as well?" Bell asked.

"That's ridiculous," Ewan shot back.

"No more ridiculous than you pining for her," Phillip replied.

Ewan frowned. His friends were confusing him. This had all seemed so tidy before they began speaking. Thea had been at his house a few weeks, she'd left, she'd refused to marry him, he was bloody well getting his life back to normal. But now they were pointing out that he missed her, and the word 'love' had been bandied about, for Christ's sake. It was far too much, too fast to think about.

"I think you should pay her a visit," Phillip said next. "See how she's doing? Ask after her leg."

Ewan poked his tongue into his cheek and glared at his friend. "After the scandal in the papers, I hardly think paying her a call would be a good idea. Besides, who is to say she'd even accept a call from me?"

Bell shrugged. "There's only one way to find out."

"No," Ewan snapped. "Paying her a call is a *very* bad idea."

"Why don't you invite her here to visit Alabaster, then?" Phillip asked.

"Who's Alabaster?" Bell asked.

"A horse," Phillip replied. "A horse Lady Thea loves very much."

"I'm certain she wouldn't come," Ewan replied. "She'd want to allow time for the scandal to die down."

"Well, there must be some way to visit her, to see her," Bell said, plucking at his bottom lip.

Ewan opened his mouth to reply just as a knock sounded on the study door. Humbolt opened the door and stepped inside. "My apologies, my lord, but you asked me to bring you any correspondence from Blackstone Hall immediately."

Ewan glanced at his friends who were both giving him knowing looks and waggling their eyebrows.

The butler held out the silver salver with the letter atop and Ewan snatched it up. "Thank you, Humbolt."

Humbolt bowed and took his leave.

Ewan ripped open the letter, ignoring the curious stares of both his friends.

"Well, what does it say?" Bell finally asked after Ewan had had ample time to read it.

Sighing, Ewan tossed the letter onto the desktop and leaned back in his chair again. "It's my invitation to the annual Christmastide ball at Blackstone Hall. I receive one every year. It's nothing special."

"It may not be special, but it's certainly convenient," Phillip replied with a wide grin.

"I never go to the Christmastide ball at Blackstone Hall. I'm usually in London," Ewan replied.

Setting his water glass on the end of the desk, Bell stood. "First, I fully intend to investigate who shared the rumor of Lady Thea's stay here with the *Times*." The marquess walked around the desk, and slapped Ewan on the back. "Second, I'd say you should change your plans this year, old man." He picked up the invitation and handed it back to Ewan. "You're going to that ball."

# CHAPTER THIRTY-SIX

*The Earl of Blackstone's Estate, December 23, 1812*

T he ballroom at Blackstone Hall was ablaze with the light of dozens of candles set in enormous chandeliers that hung above the large room. The entire ballroom was strung with evergreen and pine boughs and it smelled like a wintry forest inside. The ballroom was filled with all of Thea's neighbors, gentry and aristocrats from all across Devon. The ladies were wearing their finest winter ballgowns, the gentlemen were wearing their best evening attire, and everyone appeared to be having a splendid time.

Everyone except Thea.

Despite the gossip, Father had insisted on hosting their annual party for their friends and neighbors. The talk had died down in the weeks since Thea had left Clayton's house. Thea leg had healed, and she was walking again (thankfully *sans* limp).

Tonight, she was dressed in a gown of white with a large green velvet bow around her waist and a white fur shrug around her shoulders. Her hair was piled atop her head and

Maggie had stuck in a whimsical bit of mistletoe. Thea was smiling and nodding and pretending to be happy, but inside she was empty.

She had been empty for weeks now. She'd told herself it was because of her ruined reputation, but given the fact that they'd received not so much as one regret to the ball on the basis of the so-called scandal, it seemed their little family had weathered the storm even more successfully than Anthony had predicted.

The *Times* had never again mentioned a thing about her, and Lord Clayton hadn't been mentioned either. The gossip may have died down, but that didn't keep the partygoers from discussing the matter. Thea had heard the odd whisper here and there throughout the night. Whispers that always seemed to disappear when she walked past.

Thea had just taken a break from standing near the double doors that led into the ballroom where she'd been greeting the guests as they entered. Father had taken over the task for the time being. They were still behaving like no more than polite strangers to one another, but at least they weren't arguing.

Thea had wandered to the refreshment table to fetch a glass of lemonade. She kept her most hostesslike smile pinned to her face, but the stares and raised brows that greeted her told her that she remained the object of gossip. To feel less conspicuous, she took her glass to stand beside a potted palm near the wall. She would happily have climbed behind the thing and disappeared if it were large enough. Moments later, to her immense relief, Anthony joined her.

"You look beautiful this evening, Sister," he said, bowing to her.

Thea returned her brother's wide smile and graced him with a curtsy. "And you look as handsome as usual," she replied in kind.

Anthony turned to stare at the crowd with her, their backs to the wall. "Seems we have a fine turnout."

Thea nodded slowly. "Yes, but everyone is whispering behind their hands."

Anthony arched a brow. "Everyone? Are you quite certain? It doesn't look like Lord Mayfeather is whispering."

Thea had to laugh when she looked at the curmudgeonly Lord Mayfeather. The man must have been nearing ninety years old and he was blind as a bat. "He can't see me well enough to whisper," Thea replied. "But I assure you, plenty of the other guests are whispering."

"Let them whisper," Anthony replied. "Would you like me to spike your lemonade with something a bit more potent? Then you won't care if they're whispering."

"Please do," Thea replied, handing him her glass.

Anthony surreptitiously turned his back on the ballroom, retrieved a flask from one of the inner pockets of his evening coat, and poured some of its contents into her lemonade glass. "There you are, dear sister. Merry Christmastide."

"Thank you, Anthony. You are a kind brother," she replied with a laugh, lifting her glass and taking a sip. She winced at the bitter contents, but continued to gamely sip. "Perhaps this will make my future conversation with Lady Hepplewhite less awful." Lady Hepplewhite was the largest gossip in Devon, and everyone knew it. No doubt she was the one fueling the whispers.

"Lady Hepplewhite is here?" Anthony glanced around the room sharply. "Where?"

"She's standing near the musicians' dais," Thea replied, refusing to look herself. "No doubt instructing them as to how to play their instruments."

Anthony chuckled. "Well, if you can withstand a conversation with her, that will be the worst of it, I'm afraid."

"I assure you, I don't look forward to it." Thea turned her

attention toward the front of the ballroom to see who else had arrived. Her gaze roved around several new faces, until—

She gasped. She froze. She clutched her brother's arm.

"Anthony," she managed to choke out in a strangled whisper.

Anthony bent down to hear her better, his brow furrowed. "Yes, what is it?"

"Why is *Lord Clayton* here?" And it was indeed Clayton. He was standing near the entrance talking to Father, smiling and laughing. Clayton wore impeccable black evening attire with a white shirt, white cravat, and white satin waistcoat. He was so handsome she felt it in her knees, which trembled. She clutched at her brother's strong arm for support.

Anthony turned to follow her gaze. He expelled a sigh. "I was afraid he might come."

"What? You knew he was invited?" Thea tried to keep her rising panic from her voice, but she knew she had failed.

"He's invited every year, Thea. He's our neighbor. He just doesn't usually attend. He prefers to spend Christmastide in London. Or has in the past at least. I thought you knew. Didn't you see the guest list this year?"

"Father told me Mrs. Lowry was handling it. With my injury, he told me not to worry about the party this year other than playing hostess when the time came." Thea was trying to get her breathing back to rights, but it was becoming more and more difficult as Clayton's blue gaze swung around the ballroom and seemed to locate her immediately. Their eyes locked. Thea's heart pounded in her chest so hard it hurt.

"Why has he come this year?" she asked Anthony, unable to stop staring at Clayton.

"I don't know," Anthony replied. "I am surprised to see him here. I do hope Father didn't encourage it."

"I hope so too." Thea downed the contents of her spiked lemonade and handed the empty glass to her brother. She waited for the drink to burn its way into her belly and for Ewan to move on from her father's company near the door, then she made her move. Keeping a false smile plastered to her face, she trailed to where her father held court near entrance to the ballroom and touched his sleeve. "May I speak to you for a moment, Father," she said in her most-pleasant voice, drawing her father away from the company.

"Yes, of course, dear," Father replied, his own false smile plastered to his face. In front of company, they were nothing but polite to each other.

Thea drew her father out into the corridor and into the sitting room near the foyer before shutting the door behind them. Thankfully, the room was empty of guests. A few candles burned in candlesticks spaced throughout the room.

"Lord Clayton is here," she said simply to her father's impatiently inquiring look.

"Yes, I know. I invited him," Father replied succinctly.

Thea tried to keep her face blank and to remove the emotion from her voice. "Why could you possibly have thought it was a good idea to invite him after the scandal?"

Her father gave her a long-suffering look. "Theodora, I honestly thought it would be more scandalous to choose *not* to invite him. He usually sends his regrets."

She swallowed the growing lump in her throat and pushed an errant curl behind her ear. "Did he say *why* he decided to come *this* year?"

"He did not," Father replied, giving her a tight smile. "And I did not ask him. However, given the assistance he's been to our family this year, it would have been beyond rude of me to have left him off the guest list."

"I suppose that's one way to look at it," Thea allowed,

running a gloved hand down her middle. It did nothing to quell the rioting nerves in her belly, however.

"It's the *only* way to look at it," Father retorted. "Now, if you'll excuse me. I intend to return to my guests. I assume you'll be able to gather yourself and return to the ballroom momentarily?"

She nodded curtly. Once. "Yes. Of course. But I daresay Clayton's presence here will only serve to stir up more gossip."

Her father paused with his fingers on the door handle. He did not look back at her. "I've no intention of asking him to leave, Theodora. If you don't wish to stir up gossip, I suggest you steer clear of him."

# CHAPTER THIRTY-SEVEN

After her father left the drawing room, Thea spent the next few moments trying to gather her thoughts. She began by taking a deep breath and folding her hands together in front of her. She shook her head slightly. She mustn't make a bigger deal about this than she already had. If she were to purposely steer clear of the viscount, it would seem as if she had something to hide. Instead, she would re-enter the ballroom, greet him as she would any other guest, and continue about her business. Yes, that was precisely how she should handle the fact that Lord Clayton was standing in her ballroom even now, looking more handsome than Adonis come to life.

*Good plan. Quite solid.* She straightened her shoulders and ran a hand down the front of her gown once more. Then she poked the mistletoe back into her coiffure more tightly.

She turned toward the door and began to walk toward it when it unexpectedly opened and Viscount Clayton himself slipped inside.

"There you are," he said, expelling his breath.

Thea swallowed hard. Up close, he was even more handsome than she remembered. His blond hair slicked back, one roguish lock left to hang over an eye. And heaven help a saint, those eyes. Blue, hooded, full of sin. She'd forgotten how compelling his eyes were.

Instinctively, she took a step back. She was supposed to be avoiding him. This wasn't good, and they *certainly* shouldn't be *alone* together.

"We must leave this room immediately," she said, her voice growing high and thin.

Ewan nodded. "I must talk to you first. Briefly. Alone."

"That's not a good idea," Thea insisted.

He reached out toward her. "Please, Thea. Just for a moment."

It was the use of her name that affected her the most. And the look in his eye, and the memory of the time they'd spent together, laughing and talking over dinner. And the scent of his spicy cologne. Oh, everything about him affected her. She couldn't help it.

All of it combined in an instant to make Thea glance behind him at the door and say, "Very well, but please make it quick. If we're seen together alone, there will be no coming back from the gossip."

He nodded once and stepped toward her. She stepped back again.

He wrinkled his brow. "Are you frightened of me?"

"Of course not," she said, but she was trembling. How could she tell him she was frightened of herself? Of her reaction to him? Of his nearness. She couldn't trust herself. The memory of their kiss in the stables at Clayton Manor came flooding back, heating her cheeks. The alcohol she'd consumed wasn't helping either. *The man is engaged. The man is engaged. The man is engaged and always has been.* If she could just keep that thought foremost in her mind, she might just escape this room with her heart intact. She shook her head and met his gaze. "What do you want to say to me?"

⁓

EWAN GAZED AT THEA. It was so good to see her again. She was a vision come to life tonight. Her dark hair piled high atop her head. The gorgeous white gown flowing down her lithe body, her pink cheeks and red lips and flashing gray eyes. He'd missed her, he realized. Her company. The way she made everything more interesting simply by being present. What did he want to say to her? So many things he didn't know where to begin. But he knew he must speak quickly. He was putting her reputation in danger being in here with her alone. He'd come here tonight for a reason.

"I must ask you one question, Thea. An important one."

She nodded and averted her gaze, turning her head to the side. "Very well."

Her profile was every bit as striking as her face. The outline of her long, graceful neck was visible in the candlelight. Her pulse hammered at the base of her throat. She was nervous. So was he.

Ewan took a deep breath. This wouldn't be an easy question to ask. But he *had* to know the answer. "Why did you refuse to marry me?"

Her throat worked as she swallowed, and she turned her gaze back to meet his. "Why would you ask me that? I thought it would be quite obvious."

He clenched his jaw. "It wasn't. Not to me."

She wrapped her arms around her middle and turned toward the mantel, her back toward him. "I refuse to allow idle gossip to dictate my life."

Ewan stalked toward her and spun her around to face him. He stared down into her eyes. Was it his imagination or was there a sheen of unshed tears there? "I don't believe you. You're not telling the truth. At least not all of it." He wanted to see her face when she lied to him.

Thea's nostrils flared. She raised her chin to meet his gaze. "Very well. Let me be more blunt. I did not want to marry a man I do not love."

Ewan dropped her arm and stepped back quickly as if she'd just struck him. He swallowed the large lump that had been forming in his throat since he'd begun speaking. He gritted his teeth. He would not allow her to see how her words had hurt him. Of course she didn't love him. She'd been forced to stay at his house to heal from a broken bone. They'd spent some time together. He'd kissed her once. That hardly meant they'd fallen in love. He'd been a fool to think she might have more intimate feelings toward him than she did.

"Of course," he breathed. "I understand. I shall not bother you again."

Thea reached a hand toward him. Her voice softened. "It's not that I don't appreciate all that you've done—"

Ewan shook his head slightly. "You needn't say more." He turned toward the door, about to walk away from her. He could live the rest of his life—he *would* live the rest of his life—without seeing Lady Theodora Ballard ever again.

But her hand on his wrist stopped him. "Ewan, wait—"

Without thinking, he whirled around and pulled her into his arms. His lips crushed down on hers and he kissed her with all the passion he felt for her. He may never speak to her again, but he would have this one last kiss to remember her by.

To his utter surprise, she kissed him back. It was more than he'd ever hoped for, but she wrapped her arms tightly around his neck and lifted up on tiptoes, kissing him back with every bit as much ardor as he'd demonstrated.

His hands moved to her hair. Then they cupped her face and kept her mouth glued to his. He stroked her cheek enjoying ever little sob, every little groan she made in the back of her throat as his tongue plunged into her mouth again and again. He turned her sharply and pushed her back against the nearby wall, needing to get closer to her, to touch her. He broke the contact of their mouths only momentarily to reach down and pull up her skirts. His hand on her thigh gave him an instant cockstand. The soft, warm skin bared to his hand made him tremble.

Thea gasped at his touch, but she did not stop him. Instead, when his mouth found hers again, her tongue met his with equal force. His mouth moved to her cheek, her temple, her ear as his hands skimmed up her legs, above her stockings. His palm cupped first her bare hip and then moved around to her buttocks, pulling her tight against him. Thea gasped against his mouth, her head tipping back and her eyes closing. Ewan was rock-hard. He ached for her.

His lips were on her throat, sucking her, tasting her, when the door to the drawing room swung open.

"I could have sworn I saw them come in here," came a female voice.

Ewan immediately dropped Thea's skirts and stepped away from her, but not before Lady Hepplewhite and her daughter saw them. The ladies' eyes were round as carriage wheels and in just a moment's time, the expression on Lady Hepplewhite's face turned from aghast shock to unmitigated glee.

"Oh, my dear," Lady Hepplewhite said to her daughter, pushing the girl back out the door, "do close your eyes. It seems as if we've just stumbled upon Lord Clayton and Lady Theodora in a *most* compromising position."

# CHAPTER THIRTY-EIGHT

Two hours later, Thea sat in her bedchamber atop her bed, her hair disheveled, her ballgown wrinkled, and the mistletoe that had once rested in her coiffure, thrown to the floor. She stared at the offensive little flower as if it were responsible for her trouble.

What in heaven's name had she been thinking? Yes, Ewan had come into the sitting room, and yes, she should have insisted they both leave immediately, but she'd been the one to grab his wrist and worse, she'd been the one who didn't push him away when he kissed her. Not only did she fail to push him away, she leaned up on tiptoes for heaven's sake. Tiptoes weren't employed by accident!

She'd wrapped her foolish arms around his blasted neck and lifted herself up in order to kiss him more soundly for the love of all that was holy. And if that wasn't reckless enough, she hadn't just allowed him to pull up her skirts and touch her, she'd *welcomed* it. There was no doubt about it. She was fully one half to blame for the ensuing chaos.

Lady Hepplewhite had wasted no time in retreating from the room with her daughter in tow and spreading the tale of what she'd witnessed all across the ballroom. Thea had waited for the lady to go before she'd run from the room and up the back staircase to her bedchamber. As usual, she'd asked Maggie to go listen at doors to find out what was happening.

"Lord Clayton has been in your father's study this entire time and your father is on the way up here," Maggie had reported moments earlier before slipping away into the adjoining room to give Thea privacy for the reckoning with her father.

This time there was no knock. Her father opened her bedchamber door with such force it bounced against the far wall. Thea winced.

He stalked into the room, pure anger on his face. "Theodora," his voice boomed. "I refuse to argue or negotiate with you. I've just come from the study where Lord Clayton and I have *signed* the marriage contract. The wedding will take place directly after Twelfth Night. Prepare yourself to marry. I don't care if I have to lock you in this room until then."

He glared at her, no doubt ready for her to argue with him, to refuse. But Thea knew what she'd done. She no longer had the refuge of righteousness or anger. She'd been a full party to this. And she was about to ruin her own life and Clayton's as a result.

"Very well, Father," she replied, absently kicking at the discarded mistletoe with her stockinged foot. She forced herself to lift her head and meet her father's disapproving stare.

Her father narrowed his eyes on her, clearly not trusting her display of acquiescence. "You agree?"

"Yes." She nodded slowly. "I know what I've done, and I am ready to accept the consequences."

She couldn't muster much sympathy for Clayton this

time, however, he *had* kissed her. She had warned him that they should leave the room. Obviously, they were attracted to each other. That was something. It might not be enough to base a marriage upon, but at least they would have that.

But she couldn't stop hearing her mother's words in her head. She was going to marry a man who didn't love her. She felt as if she would retch.

"Very well," Father retorted, obviously willing to leave well enough alone. "I shall inform Maggie that you should prepare your *trousseau*. Tomorrow we can discuss the details of the marriage contract."

"Fine," Thea replied, staring unseeing at the wall.

Father retreated quickly from the room, leaving Thea to fall back upon the bed and curl into a small ball. Oh, why had Ewan come here tonight? He'd said he had an important question to ask her. He'd asked her why she'd refused to marry him. Could it be that his pride was hurt? She'd told him the first thing that had come to mind, that she refused to allow gossip to ruin her life. He'd essentially called her a liar, forcing her to tell him something that he would find more believable. "I did not want to marry a man I do not love," she'd shot back at him. The look on his face had been hurt. That surprised her. The truth—that she couldn't bring herself to tell him—was she didn't want to marry a man who didn't love *her*. But now, *now* she was going to do just that, and no amount of guilt or recrimination would make that untrue.

# CHAPTER THIRTY-NINE

Ewan stood at the altar of the little village church as Thea walked down the aisle toward him. He hadn't seen her since the night of the Christmastide ball. Both he and Lord Blackstone had agreed that would be for the best. Blackstone had sent word, however, that Thea was willing to marry him. Apparently, she agreed that after Lady Hepplewhite's gossip, there was no other choice. An unconfirmed story in the *Times* was one thing. Lady Hepplewhite and her daughter seeing it with their own eyes was quite another.

Thea walked toward Ewan looking as if she were walking toward an executioner. She looked small. Small and frightened, almost like a little girl. The bouquet of winter lilies she held in her hands was trembling slightly and her mouth remained a thin, unhappy line as she made her way to stand beside him.

The church was nearly empty on this cold, January morning. Lord Blackstone, Anthony, Maggie, and Lord Theodore Harding, Thea's uncle, stood at the pews on Thea's side. Only Bell and Dr. Blanchard stood on Ewan's side. Dr. Blanchard had only taken his side to even out the guests. Bell had been the only one of Ewan's oldest friends who had been able to make it on such short notice. As a Naval officer, Kendall was out of the country and Worth was indisposed. Phillip couldn't attend and risk being recognized. Ewan's own mother hadn't traveled to Devon from London due to the cold. Instead, she'd sent him a letter asking him to bring his new bride to the city for a visit the first chance he got.

Meanwhile, the vicar spoke the words that would bind Ewan and Thea together for life and Thea didn't even glance at him. Instead, she kept her eyes trained on the vicar, a half-stunned, half-resigned look on her face. It was as if she were attending a funeral instead of her own wedding.

Guilt pummeled Ewan's conscience with every word the clergyman spoke. Ewan was forcing a young woman to marry him. A young woman who clearly didn't want him. She'd said as much. She hadn't wanted him after the gossip about them appeared in the *Times* and she didn't want him now. The only difference was, now she was trapped. And he'd been the one to trap her. Not on purpose, never that. But he'd been the one who'd followed her to the drawing room, waited for her father to leave, and then forced her to speak to him. She'd even told him she wanted to leave the room, precisely because she was fearful they'd be seen together. But Ewan *insisted* she stay. There was no doubt in his mind that he was entirely to blame for what happened between them that night and he was ruining this poor young woman's life by forcing her into an unwanted marriage.

Ewan, too, kept his eyes trained on the vicar, repeating the words that sealed their fate. When it was over, when they were well and truly married and had signed the record book, they turned to face their friends. Their faces completely blank, they promptly left the altar in opposite directions.

~

THE WEDDING PARTY piled into three different coaches to return to Ewan's estate. The wedding breakfast was a tense and awkward affair held in the dining room at Clayton Manor. Dr. Blanchard and Lord Theodore did their best to keep the conversation going. Meanwhile, Ewan cleared his throat uncomfortably, Thea poked at her meal without consuming a bite, and Anthony and Lord Blackstone drank brandy at ten o'clock in the morning. Bell simply observed the whole affair with a good-natured friendliness that no one appreciated.

After the breakfast had mercifully ended, all of the guests, except Bell and Maggie, took their leave. Ewan and Thea walked everyone to the door. Lord Blackstone kissed his daughter on the cheek without saying a word, while Anthony clapped Ewan on the shoulder. "Congratulations, old man. Best of luck." Then he hugged his sister and slipped out the door.

Lord Theodore made a long, unwieldy speech about how proud he was of his only niece for having married at last. Then he welcomed Ewan into the family. Ewan did his best to be gracious, while wishing the older man would simply take his leave.

Immediately after the door closed behind the group, Thea turned to Ewan with a stonelike look on her face and said, "I should greatly like to take a nap."

"Of course. It's been a long morning," Ewan replied with an equal lack of emotion. He had no objection to her plan. How could he? He was trapped somewhere between wanting to take a nap himself and wanting to join Bell in the study and drink. After Thea had disappeared up the staircase, Ewan opted for the latter.

THE MOMENT EWAN entered the study, Bell held up a glass. The marquess was already sitting in front of Ewan's desk with a brandy glass filled for him. His own ubiquitous water glass at the ready. "Congratulations, Clayton! I know I speak for Kendall and Worth as well when I say we'd never have thought *you'd* be the first to tie the parson's noose around your neck."

Ewan readily took the glass from his friend and walked around his desk to sit. "Really? Who did you think would be first?"

"I suppose I always thought it would be Kendall," Bell replied. "He'll need a countess sooner or later, now that he's an earl."

Ewan nodded slowly. Their group of friends all knew that Kendall, who'd been a second son at the time, had been tossed over by a young woman who had received an offer of marriage from a baron. It had greatly affected Kendall. The man hadn't attempted to court another lady since. But now that his brother had died and he was the earl, Kendall wouldn't have the luxury of remaining a bachelor. "I suppose you're right," Ewan agreed. He tugged at his cravat to loosen the thing. He was convinced it had been about to choke him all morning.

"But there's plenty of time for all of that," Bell continued, raising his glass in the air for a toast. "Here's to you and your new viscountess. May you have decades of happiness together."

Ewan dutifully raised his glass and drank, but he highly doubted he and Thea would have decades of happiness. Not given the way their marriage had begun.

Ewan spent the next several hours trying to drink away the memory of the unhappy look on Thea's face as she'd marched down the aisle toward him this morning. He'd ruined her life today. She'd called him an ass the day they'd met. She was bloody well right.

≈

BY THE TIME Ewan took his leave from Bell that evening, he was not nearly inebriated enough. Oh, he'd drunk enough. Plenty. But he still had his wits about him. The only thing that could make him more of an ass on his wedding night would be being a *drunken* ass. And he had no intention of making Thea's day any worse.

To that end, he'd waited long enough. He'd remained in the study with Bell for hours. It was well past dinner time. He'd hidden from his new wife long enough. No matter what happened between them tonight, it was time for the reckoning.

"Good night, old chap," he said, standing, walking around his desk, and clapping Bell on the shoulder.

"Good night," Bell replied, lifting the last sip of his water in the air. "I do believe I'll go to bed myself. But first I'll stop in the library and get something to read."

As Ewan climbed the stairs to his bedchamber, he found himself envying his friend for his ability to simply climb into his bed and read tonight. Ewan, however, had to go have what was certain to be an awkward conversation with his new wife about how they intended to spend their wedding night. The irony was not lost on him.

Ewan entered his bedchamber and quietly closed the door behind him. His gaze immediately fell on the door that joined his room to Thea's. She had to be in the adjoining bedchamber. Was she expecting him to come to her or did she want nothing to do with him? He ripped his cravat from around his neck and scrubbed a hand through his hair. He wasn't just an ass. He was also a fool. A man should go to his wife on their wedding night. Instead, he was hemming and hawing in his room like an untried school lad.

First, he divested himself of his coat, waistcoat and cravat. Then he spent an inordinate amount of time pulling off his boots and stockings, then he crossed his arms behind his neck and pulled off his shirt.

Wearing only his breeches, he paced toward her door. He paced away. He cursed himself for a fool a half dozen times.

The faintest knock sounded on the door between their bedchambers. "Come in," he called, the breath catching in his throat.

The door opened slowly, and Thea stood there in a filmy concoction of white lace that made her look positively delectable. Her long, dark hair was down around her shoulders and the nightrail she was wearing was nearly see-through. Ewan's throat went dry. Sweat beaded on his forehead. He gulped.

She walked barefooted into his bedchamber with tentative steps and tossed her hair across her shoulders before looking directly at him and saying, "Should we get this over with?"

# CHAPTER FORTY

Thea felt like an idiot. She was wearing the most ridiculous frothy ensemble of lace and gossamer she'd ever seen. And of course it was *white* of all embarrassing colors. Days ago, Maggie had attempted to involve her in the choice of her wedding night attire, but Thea's only response had been a glare. She'd left the details to Maggie, who, of course had never *had* a wedding night, and so it was Thea's own fault that she was now dressed like a confection, standing in front of Ewan looking like a powdered puff pastry.

She might not know much about marriage, but she knew enough to know that married people were supposed to spend their wedding night together. In bed. She'd spent the last few hours with a litany of questions scrolling through her mind: Would Ewan even want to bed her? Or was he still angry with her for ruining his plans with his *fiancée*? Who *was* his *fiancée*? Did Thea even want to know? Probably not. Knowing the identity of the woman Ewan truly wanted was certain to only make the thought of it that much more excruciating. No doubt his former *fiancée* was an accomplished debutante. A darling of the *ton*. Not a stubborn aged spinster who lived in Devon, was obsessed with a horse, and wore clothing such as this ridiculous puffy nightrail.

It took a few moments before Thea realized that Ewan was standing in the glow of the candles wearing only his breeches. The firelight flickered over his bare chest. She allowed her gaze to travel from his slightly mussed hair, across his wide, square shoulders, down the thick muscles of his arms, to the flat plane of his abdomen. She swallowed, hard. The man was even better looking with no shirt on. *Hmm.* She hadn't expected that.

Ewan's blue gaze narrowed upon her. "Did you just ask me if we should 'get this over with'?"

Thea winced. She'd been doing her best not to wring her hands since she'd stepped inside the room. She was not a handwringer, and she refused to become one, even over something as excruciating as this. Handwringing was Maggie's *forte*. "Yes?" she finally offered. "That's what I said."

Ewan's response was to burst into laughter. Oh, *that* made her feel better. She was supposed to be seductive, instead she was laughable. For an interminable moment, she considered turning and fleeing, but that would be the coward's way out. And she had no intention of being a coward tonight or any night. She sucked a deep breath into her lungs and straightened her shoulders.

"I suppose it is funny," she allowed, glancing down at her attire, "especially this nightrail."

"No." Ewan shook his head. He strode to her and placed his hands on her shoulders. The warmth from his touch sent a shudder through her. "You look absolutely gorgeous, Thea. I was laughing at your words, not at you."

"Yes, well, I'm not exactly trained in the art of seduction," she said with another half-smile.

He returned her smile, lifting one hand to softly rub her

cheek. "Unfortunately, neither am I. Would you like to just talk?"

Relief flooded through her and she silently nodded.

Ewan captured her hand and led her to the bed. They sat together on the edge of the enormous mattress, which was covered with a dark blue satin blanket. She spent a few moments looking around the huge room. It was dim in the bedchamber, but she could see enough to know it looked like him in here. The furnishings were a mixture of dark blues and grays and browns. Everything was in its place. A very *conventional* bedchamber.

It smelled like him in here too. A mixture of spice and soap and something indefinable that even now made her want to curl into him and lick his neck for some reason. Oh, for heaven's sake, what was wrong with her? Why was she thinking about neck licking?

"I never expected us to be here," Ewan began. He still held her hand in his and when he finished speaking, he squeezed it. His warm fingers engulfing her cold ones.

Thea squeezed back, but tears stung the backs of her eyes. He meant that he never expected *her* to be here. He was wishing she was someone else. They both knew it. But she had to put that out of her mind, had to forget about it...for tonight at least.

Ewan turned to face her. "Thea, I—"

She pushed herself up against the mattress on her free hand and touched her lips to his, silencing him.

THEA'S KISS was all the encouragement Ewan needed. He'd expected they would talk for a while. He wasn't even entirely certain they would be intimate. He definitely hadn't been ready to make love to a woman who had begun the night by asking, "Should we get this over with?" But he should have known that beautiful, courageous Thea wouldn't do anything less than give herself to him completely on their wedding night. Just touching her made him shudder. He wanted to make this good for her. He wanted to make it extraordinary.

Ewan pulled her into his arms and opened his mouth on hers. He cupped the back of her head to pull her closer. Her tongue flicked out to touch his…tentative at first and then, when his tongue went deeper, hers matched his thrust for thrust.

He pushed her back onto the mattress and leaned down over her. He glanced down her body at her nightrail. "How much do you love this garment?"

"I hate it," she murmured, smiling up at him.

"Then you won't mind if I do this?" He grabbed the bodice and ripped the fabric from top to bottom in one decisive move. "There. That's better." His eyes devoured her.

Thea helped him as he pulled the remaining bits from her shoulders and she laid there, completely naked and perfect on his bed. His fantasies had never been this good. Her legs were long, and her hips curved, her breasts beyond imagination. Her skin was like silk.

He loomed above her, both arms braced tight against the mattress on either side of her head. He leaned down and kissed her again, stoking the fire inside of both of them. Thea cried out when he pulled his head away. But when he moved down to her bare breasts and took her nipple in his mouth, she cried out again, this time, his name. Would he ever tire of hearing his name on her lips that way? He gently bit her nipple, cupping her full breast in his hand, then he sucked the little bud sharply into his mouth. Thea gasped. Her chest heaved against him from her rasping breaths and her hands tangled in his hair. "Ewan," she cried again. He smiled against her soft skin.

He took his time, lavishing attention first on one taut nipple, then the next, sucking, nibbling, pulling the hard little bud into his mouth and biting ever so softly until Thea was writhing beneath him. Her hands still tangling in his hair, her hips undulating beneath him telling him she wanted something she didn't even know about.

"Ewan," she breathed. "I ache."

He closed his eyes against the desire to whip off his breeches and bury himself inside of her. "So do I." He knew what she wanted, what she needed, and he had every intention of giving it to her before he took his own pleasure.

He let his hand wander down her tense leg to slowly move back up toward her hip. He stroked the outside of her thigh. Kissing her deeply again, he cupped her hip and let his hand ride there for a few moments before moving his fingers between her legs. He brushed against her curls lightly, once, before sliding one finger into her wet warmth.

Thea nearly came off the bed. He moved his mouth to her ear, quieting her. "Shh, darling. Don't worry. Let me touch you like this."

Her hips were still undulating against his hand. And when he slipped his finger back inside of her, she moaned. Then his thumb found the nub of pleasure between her thighs and he knew pure bliss watching her expressive face while her eyes rolled back into her head as she murmured "please" again and again.

"I want to taste you," he whispered in her ear sensing that instead of being frightened by his words, she would be excited by them.

"Yes," she whispered back, and Ewan couldn't help the self-satisfied grin that spread across his lips as he moved down her body.

He slid a second finger into her tight sheath and her eyes widened in shock for one instant before she tossed her head back and moaned. He moved his fingers within her, stroking her, making her more wet, before he continued to move down her body, breathing in her intoxicating scent. He was obsessed with her. Couldn't get enough of her.

He circled his thumb, once, twice, and her hips arched off the mattress before he replaced his thumb with the tip of his tongue. Thea's breath caught in her throat. Her knees fell apart giving him more access. He dipped his head and licked her. She moaned. He licked her again. Her hips bucked. Another deep wet lick.

"Do you like this?" he asked, raising his head to look up at her over the plane of her flat belly.

Her lips moved, but she couldn't seem to form the word. All she could do was nod and mouth the word 'yes'.

He smiled to himself as he bent his head back to his task. He was going to make her come with his tongue. And it was going to be a *pleasure*.

THEA GASPED when Ewan's tongue touched her once more. The ungodly ache between her legs made her hips arch off the mattress. She'd never imagined anything like what he was doing to her, but she never wanted him to stop. He stroked her with his tongue again and again and the rough brush of it made her cry out, "Don't stop."

Thankfully, he didn't. Instead, his hands cupped her buttocks, holding her hips in place as he licked her even more deeply between the folds of her sex. Just when she thought she could bear no more, the tip of his tongue flicked across that most sensitive spot again and again in such unmercifully cruel nonstop licks that she clenched her jaw and groaned.

Her hands reached down to tug at him, her fingers tangling in his blond hair. "Ewan, I—" She wasn't entirely certain what she wanted to say, and tears welled her eyes, which made no sense.

His tongue kept up the strokes until she was so wet the sheets dampened beneath her. Her breathing hitched and her vision blurred and finally, finally, a thousand sparks of light and pleasure exploded beneath her eyelids as the most amazing feeling she'd ever felt radiated out in pulsing waves from that tiny spot he'd been licking to throb throughout her thighs and her legs.

Afterward, she lay in a crumpled heap, her breathing heavy, her heart pounding, not knowing what to do next. What in the name of everything had that man just done to her? If this was what all wedding nights were like, then young ladies needed to know posthaste. They wouldn't be interested in remaining spinsters if all gentlemen knew how to do what Ewan had just done.

He lifted himself above her, bracing himself on his muscled forearms, looking down at her with a grin on his face that told her he was aware of what had just happened to her. And that he was awfully proud of it.

"What was that?" she breathed, putting the back of her hand to her forehead. Her entire body felt limp. Limp and simply wonderful.

"That was an orgasm," he said simply. "At least I believe that's the scientific name for it."

"What's the unscientific name for it?" she asked with a laugh.

He leaned over and whispered the naughty word in her ear. She laughed again, moving her hand down to cover her hammering heart. "Whatever you call it, it was wonderful."

"I'm glad you enjoyed it," he replied.

"That's an understatement." Her body was still zinging with pleasure and she was still trying to get her breathing back to rights.

"What if I told you there's more," he announced, nuzzling her ear.

Thea pushed herself up on her elbow to stare at him as if he was a magical creature. "What? How can there possibly be more?"

"Well," he chuckled. "I *am* still wearing my breeches."

Thea's entire body turned pink. He watched it happen. First her face and hairline and then the lovely color spread all the way down to her toes. It was absolutely adorable.

She clapped a hand over her mouth and mumbled, "I'm a fool. I'm an idiot. I'm—"

"You're none of those things," he insisted. He shifted onto his side and reached out to curl a strand of her long hair around his finger. When he spoke, his voice was soft, caring. "Thea," he asked. "How much did your mother ever tell you about lovemaking?"

Her brow furrowed into confusion. "Lovemaking?" she echoed.

"Or what happens between a husband and wife…in bed?" Ewan clarified.

Thea winced. "Mama never really had much of a chance to explain…" She trailed off, obviously mortified.

Ewan winced too. "And I'm guessing your father and your brother never told you anything about it."

She shook her head vigorously, her cheeks still bright pink. "Nothing," she breathed.

"Very well. I'll show you. Don't worry."

She swallowed hard. "You telling me not to worry makes me worry."

Ewan chuckled. He brushed a strand of her hair away

from her cheek. "No, darling, don't worry. I promise you don't need to." He leaned forward and captured her lips with his again.

~

AFTER A FEW MOMENTS OF KISSING, Thea felt her body begin to relax again. It was lovely kissing Ewan. He was so handsome. And if he was able to do to her body again what he'd done before, she'd kiss him forever.

He pulled his lips away from hers and traced her cheekbones with his thumbs. "You're gorgeous, Thea. Do you know that?"

She shook her head. "You don't have to say that."

His brows snapped together in a decided frown. "I would never say that if it weren't true. I was captivated by your beauty the moment I met you."

*Captivated by my beauty? Why, that sounded lovely.* She felt herself smile. "No. That cannot possibly be true."

"It's true," he murmured, kissing her again. "I promise you." He touched the tip of her nose with the tip of his.

His lips moved down to her neck and he nuzzled there while she gasped. "I thought you were handsome," she admitted.

She felt his smile against the soft skin of her neck. "Did you?" He moved his mouth to her ear and licked inside.

She gasped again. "Yes, I wanted to slap you, of course, but I couldn't deny you were handsome." She laughed.

His smile widened. Next, he lowered his head to her breast and sucked on the nipple. Then he moved his hand down between her legs. She was still wet. He teased her with his fingers for a few moments before he slipped one inside of her.

"Ewan," she cried.

"Do you like that?" he whispered huskily in her ear as he moved his finger in and out.

She bit her lip and nodded. "Um. Hum."

His finger moved inside of her and she felt the tension building in her thighs again. Oh, heavens, would she feel that wonderful feeling once more?

"I'm glad you like it, Thea, because lovemaking is just me putting myself inside of you, just like this." He pulled his finger out and slid in again.

She couldn't breathe. "Your finger?" she managed.

"Another part of me," he replied. He pulled his finger away and sat up.

Thea momentarily felt bereft. She wanted him back, wanted him touching her, kissing her, wanted his finger inside her again. Wanted his mouth on her, licking her and—

He rolled onto his back and began unbuttoning the fall of his breeches.

Thea shot up onto one arm. "Oh!"

He eyed her warily, still unbuttoning. "Oh, what?"

"I'm such a ninny," she replied, biting her lower lip. "You need to be naked of course."

His smile made her insides melt. One lock of hair had fallen over his forehead and he looked so roguishly handsome she longed to kiss him again.

"Do you want to help me?" he asked, glancing suggestively down toward his breeches.

Her eyes went round, and a smile spread across her lips. "May I?"

~

"Please do." Ewan's hands fell to either side of his hips. It was going to kill him to let her finish unbuttoning his breeches, but he *needed* to feel her soft hand on his cock.

Thea's fingers looked tiny compared to his large ones as they moved to the fall of his breeches. She pushed the fabric aside and took up where he'd left off. He'd only managed to unbutton the top two buttons. Four more to go.

Her deft fingers moved to the first button on the right. She slowly pushed the button through the fabric. She paused to watch his face.

"Go on," he encouraged, clenching his jaw against the unholy lust he was struggling to control.

She blushed beautifully and moved her hand to the button on the left. That one she unbuttoned even more slowly. His cock was throbbing. He fisted the sheets, his knuckles turning white. "You're going to kill me."

"Does this cause you pain?" she asked, watching his face with renewed interest.

"I ache for you," he breathed. Her hand was so near his cock, so tantalizingly close.

Smiling at the knowledge of her power, Thea took a deep breath and reached for the next button on the right. She pushed herself down his body until her face was only inches away from his cock. The breath abandoned Ewan's lungs. He stared up at the ceiling. "Heaven, help me."

"Help you what?" she replied with a laugh. "There is only one button left."

"I know and..." He took a long, deep, shuddering breath.

"And what?" Thea teased. Her finger circled the last button, making him mad with wanting. His cock jumped each time she brushed her finger against the fabric. How in the hell did this innocent young woman know so instinctively how to tease him?

He took another long, shuddering breath and began his

sentence again. "And I may very well unman myself if you don't hurry, love."

"I don't know what that means," she replied, pulling the final button through the final hole. "But it sounds like something that should be avoided at all costs."

"It should," he murmured, his breath coming in panting gasps as she pulled the fall of the breeches away to reveal his throbbing cock.

"God, Thea, touch me, please," he begged.

The light flutter of her fingers against him made him clench his jaw so hard it hurt. She brushed her fingers over him before they fluttered away.

"Harder, please. Squeeze me." He closed his eyes.

Her fist wrapped around him and Ewan forgot to breathe. She gripped his cock in her palm and it was a pleasure unlike any he'd known before. How did her simple touch do such things to him? "Stroke me," he pleaded.

Her hand moved up and down his length and Ewan's lips fell open. He sat there braced on his elbows while Thea made his entire body shudder. He allowed the exquisite torture for a few more agonizing moments before he grabbed her fist and pulled it from him, before leaning down to practically rip the breeches from his legs. He tossed the garment aside and took control once more, rolling Thea onto her back and covering her with the length of his naked body. His hard planes meshed with her soft curves. His mouth found hers again and their tongues tangled as Thea wrapped her arms around his neck and fit her gloriously nude body intimately against his.

Ewan groaned at the contact.

He moved his lips to her ear and whispered, "That's the part of me that will be inside of you. I want you so badly."

She glanced down at him, biting her lip. "Are you certain I shouldn't worry?"

Ewan chuckled. How did this woman make him laugh in the middle of making him mad with lust? It was an unexpected combination to be certain and one he quite enjoyed.

"Your body will expand for me. And the wetness will help," he murmured.

She nodded and took a deep breath. "All right."

Ewan closed his eyes and found her lips again in the darkness. She was trusting him. Trusting him to tell her the truth, trusting him with her body. Trusting him completely. He would not betray her trust.

He moved his hand down between her legs once more to ensure she was still ready for him. She kept her arms wrapped around his neck and closed her eyes tightly. He probed at her wet warmth before using his hand to guide his cock inside. He pushed in slightly, watching her face for any sign of discomfort. "Are you all right?" he asked, clenching his jaw against the unholy torture of being partially inside her and having to wait.

"Yes." She nodded but she didn't open her eyes. Her throat worked. He kissed it.

He pushed in a bit farther, clenching his jaw even harder. If Thea had opened her eyes, she would have seen exactly how difficult a struggle it was for him. "All right?" he asked, his voice a rough whisper.

She nodded again.

He pushed himself in to the hilt and remained still, gasping against his body's urge to move.

Thea's eyes flew open.

"Did I hurt you?" he asked, showering small kisses along her cheeks, hoping against hope that it hadn't been too awful.

"No." She shook her head. She moved a little, making him gasp. "It… it just feels so… wonderful." She closed her eyes and wrapped her arms around his neck again.

She lurched against him, sliding against his cock.

"Jesus Christ," Ewan swore under his breath.

But it was all the encouragement he needed to continue. He pulled out slowly and slid back inside, once, twice, waiting for any sign that he was hurting her. When he knew she was all right, he pumped into her over and over, hard and fast but not *too* hard, not *too* fast—there would be time for that sort of lovemaking later.

Using his thumb to rub her again, he forced himself to slow his pace while he built her lust, circling the nub between her folds until he felt her thighs go tense. Her head began tossing back and forth on the mattress and she clawed at his back, making whimpering, pleading noises in the back of her throat. It took every ounce of self-control he had, but Ewan waited until she came again beneath him, her back arching so that her breasts pressed against his chest. The muscles inside her clenched him unmercifully as he steadily thrust into her again and again, his own climax building to such a force that he pushed himself inside of her once last time and shuddered into her hot wetness, a ragged groan torn from his throat.

His weight collapsed on her for only a moment before he rolled to the side, taking her with him and cradling her against his chest, his heartbeat thundering beneath his ribs. He held her tightly against him as the sweat on his skin dried and he tried to remember his own name. Never in his life had he experienced an orgasm like that.

"You felt the same thing I felt earlier, didn't you?" she asked, a smile filled with what could only be pride resting on her full sultry lips.

All he could do was nod and pull her hand up to his lips. He kissed the center of her palm and placed it over his heart. "Do you feel what you did to me?"

Thea's eyes widened as she realized how quickly his heart was beating.

"Well, if you felt anything close to what I felt, I understand exactly why," she said.

He pulled her atop him and ran his fingers through her thick hair. "You're beautiful, Lady Clayton. And now, you are well and truly mine."

## CHAPTER FORTY-ONE

They made love two more times that night and Thea
was amazed each time at the things her body was
capable of and the things Ewan knew how to do to
elicit the responses he wanted. He knew just where to touch,
what to whisper in her ear, and when to whisper it to
heighten her pleasure. By the time dawn peeked through the
curtains, Ewan was fast asleep, and Thea was sore, satiated,
and thoroughly unnerved.

He'd called her beautiful. He'd called her Lady Clayton.
He'd even said she was 'well and truly' his. He'd done things
to her body that she had never dreamed possible. In the span
of one evening, she had the sinking suspicion that he'd
chained her to him thoroughly body and soul. After all, a
lady could fall in love with someone who called her beautiful.
She could love someone who claimed her as his. But he'd
never once mentioned the word love, not even at the height
of his pleasure.

Going to bed with Ewan tonight had seemed like the
obvious and proper thing to do. They were married and it
was their wedding night. But now that the wedding night

was over, Thea was terrified that he would leave her for a mistress in London while she'd stayed here alone night after night, with nothing but the memory of his touch. And the thought of Ewan doing the things he'd just done to her with a mistress made a pit form in Thea's stomach.

She glanced at her husband's sleeping form. He looked younger, more vulnerable, peaceful. But he was still undeniably handsome with his long eyelashes splayed against his tan cheeks. Thea pushed her palm against her forehead. Dear God, despite her best intentions, she'd done precisely what her mother had done, what her mother had *warned* her against. Thea had married a man who she felt more for than he did. She was a fool. A complete fool.

As the sun rose, Thea slipped out of Ewan's bed, grabbed up the remnants of her ridiculous nightrail, and made her way back into her own bedchamber. She shut the adjoining door behind her as quietly as possible and winced when it made a little thump. She glanced around her new bedchamber, which was even more spectacular than the one she'd had when she'd been here as a guest. She pulled a dressing gown from her wardrobe and tied it around her waist before she began pacing the floor, biting her thumbnail and trying to still her growing panic.

She had to regain control of herself and her thoughts. She and Ewan had had a lovely evening. A memorable wedding night. But she could not allow herself to think it had been any more than that. Their marriage wasn't a love match. She'd do well to remember that fact. She would get started today at the business of being a viscountess. That was her role now and she'd been raised to it. Being a lovesick wife who wanted to jump into bed the moment her husband quirked his finger was decidedly *not* in her plans.

She paced in front of the bed for a few more moments, deciding on her course of action. First, she would take a long, hot bath and a nap. Later, she would go and have tea with Phillip.

EWAN YAWNED and stretched before rolling himself over in the bed and feeling around for his wife's soft, welcoming body. He patted the space next to him for several moments before realizing that he'd managed to find nothing more than cold sheets. He sat up straight and rubbed the sleep from his eyes.

The morning light streamed through an opening in the curtains. He glanced at her side of the bed. Thea was gone. He was alone. She'd obviously slipped back into her room at some point in the night. Ewan expelled his breath and uttered a curt expletive.

Did she regret what had happened between them? Or did she simply prefer not to see him this morning? Either way he didn't like waking up without her. Regardless of their forced marriage, Ewan couldn't deny that the attraction between them was fierce. Their lovemaking last night had been extraordinary. Like nothing he'd ever experienced before. The entire evening had gone nothing like he'd expected, but it had been better than his wildest dreams.

Ewan tossed the covers aside and got out of bed. Without bothering to call his valet, Ewan pulled on some clothing and went to visit Phillip. Despite the early hour, he needed a drink. And some advice.

In that order.

PHILLIP, it turned out, was not as keen to drink before noon as Ewan happened to be. But the future duke was more than willing to sit in his friend's study and lend an ear while Ewan poured himself a glass of brandy.

"Congratulations, Clayton," Phillip said, raising a non-existent glass in Ewan's honor.

Ewan raised his own real one in salute and took a drink. "Thank you," he mumbled.

Phillip arched a brow. "If you don't mind my saying so, you look a bit…rough for a happily married bridegroom."

Ewan glanced down at his wrinkled clothing and emitted a short growl. He rubbed at the day-old stubble on his cheeks. "What does it matter?" he grumbled.

"I suppose that's one way to look at it," Phillip replied, shaking his head. "Marriage trouble already, Clayton?"

Ewan shrugged and poked out his cheek with his tongue. "Oh, not much unless one thinks one's wife hating him is trouble."

Phillip's brows snapped together. "Why in the world would you believe she hates you?"

Ewan expelled his breath in a long rush. "I ruined her life. Why *wouldn't* she hate me?"

Phillip's brow remained drawn. "*How* precisely did you ruin her life?"

"Let's see." Ewan lifted his glass again and stared at the amber liquid inside. "Thea made it quite clear she didn't want to marry me, and instead of taking no for an answer, I showed up at her house and compromised her in front of the biggest gossip in the countryside, thereby forcing her into the marriage."

Phillip's face remained skeptical. "You *forced* yourself on her? *That* doesn't sound like you, Clayton."

Ewan shrugged. "I kissed her."

Phillip chuckled. "Yes, and I assume she kissed you back if you were still kissing when the biggest gossip in the country-side entered the room."

Ewan pinched the bridge of his nose. "Yes, but if I hadn't gone looking for Thea in the sitting room, then—"

"And if Napoleon weren't such a horse's ass, we wouldn't be at war. Things happen for reasons, Clayton. And it sounds to me as if the two of you couldn't keep your hands off one another. That says something."

"I'm not certain Thea would agree with that statement," Ewan grumbled, but even as he said the words, he couldn't stop thinking of last night in bed with Thea. They certainly hadn't been able to keep their hands off each other then. *Thank God*.

Phillip crossed his arms over his chest and regarded his friend down the length of his nose. "Well, Thea is coming to have tea with me later, and I'm quite interested to hear *Lady Clayton's* side of this tale."

## CHAPTER FORTY-TWO

L ater that morning, Thea knocked lightly on the door to Phillip's sitting room. Maggie had drawn Thea a bath earlier and they hadn't spoken about any of the details of the night before. The maid might have raised her eyebrows when she gathered the remnants of the torn nightrail, but to her credit she didn't say a word. *Thank heavens*. Thea had little idea how she would have explained it had her friend asked.

Thea had been looking forward to her visit with Phillip all day. She might be married to a man who didn't love her, but at least she had Phillip to talk to and Alabaster to ride again. Things might not be so bad here at Clayton Manor after Ewan left to return to his life in London.

"Come in," came Phillip's gentle voice.

Thea pushed open the door and stepped inside. Bright sunlight streamed through the windows on the far side of the room. Phillip was sitting at his writing desk, busily scribbling. She smiled brightly at the sight of her friend. The moment he realized it was her, he turned, stood and immediately returned her smile.

"There you are, Viscountess Clayton," Phillip said. He stood and bowed to her.

Thea swallowed. This was the first time anyone had called her by her new married name. It surprised her, causing her to go silent for a moment. "Yes, I'm Viscountess Clayton now. For better or for worse."

Phillip frowned. "What does *that* mean?"

She shook her head. "It doesn't matter. It's good to see you, *Your Grace*," she finally managed.

"No. Now, there will be none of that. My name is Phillip and that's what you shall call me forevermore."

She inclined her head and smiled. "Very well...Phillip."

"It's good to see you standing and walking," he continued. "It's the first time I've seen you do that, you know."

Thea chuckled. "I suppose that's true. My leg has healed. I do hope you received my letter and have forgiven me for leaving without saying good-bye."

"Of course." Phillip cleared his throat. "I'm only sorry I couldn't come to the wedding," he said, guilt lining his features. "I hope you understand. I'm not yet ready to tell Society that I'm not dead." He chuckled.

"Funny," Thea breathed. "I sort of wish I *could* tell Society that I'm dead."

Phillip strode to her and took her hands. He studied her face. "That hardly sounds like a happy bride. Come and sit."

Tears burned the backs of Thea's eyes as she followed the duke to a set of chairs near the window and took a seat in one of them. Phillip waited for her to sit before lowering himself into the other chair.

"I'm not much of a happy bride, I'm afraid," Thea began, staring out the window at the sky.

Phillip studied her face. "I'm sorry to hear that. Tell me what happened. Clayton's only given me the barest sketch of the details."

Thea pressed her lips together and shrugged. "I suppose now that I'm a married lady, I can do things like sit and talk with you about such things."

Phillip nodded. "I only want to help. Clayton told me you'd refused to marry him after the gossip in the papers."

Thea sighed. "That's true but then…" Her cheeks burned. Why was it difficult to admit what had happened after?

"Then, what?" Phillip prompted.

"Then Ewan came to my father's Christmastide ball. And he kissed me. And I kissed him. And Lady Hepplewhite saw us."

"And you were forced to marry." Phillip searched her face. "That's why you're unhappy? You didn't want to marry Clayton?"

"No, er, not…precisely." Thea bit her lip and glanced away.

"Well, you're hardly the first couple to marry under, ahem, rushed circumstances," Phillips said.

"Yes, but normally couples who marry under such rushed circumstances are madly in love."

Phillip's brow furrowed. "Madly in love? What do you mean?"

Thea couldn't meet her friend's eyes. "Never mind. I… I don't know what I mean either. The fact is that if I hadn't sneaked here and broken my leg, Ewan wouldn't be married to a woman he never wanted."

Phillip frowned at her. "Is that what you think?"

Thea spent an inordinate amount of time staring at and smoothing her skirts before replying. "What else am I to think? He'd planned to marry another lady and now…now he's stuck with me. I've ruined his life."

"*You've* ruined *his* life?" Phillip's nose was completely wrinkled into a frown as if he were thoroughly confused.

Thea nodded miserably.

Phillip tilted his head to the side. "Seems to me that if he kissed you, Clayton has some responsibility to bear as well."

"Of course he does, but the kiss was a spontaneous mistake, obviously. He shouldn't have to scrap all his carefully made plans over it. And no wife wants to be a 'responsibility.'"

Phillip pursed his lips, opened his mouth to speak, and shut it again before finally saying, "Lady Thea, if you will allow me to speak bluntly…"

Thea swallowed and nodded some more. "By all means."

"At the risk of telling my friend's secrets, Clayton was a complete mope after you left. And that's coming from me, who has been a complete mope for months."

Thea couldn't help but laugh at her friend's description. "Phillip, you were not a mope. You were devastated. You were just back from war where you nearly died. You'd been through far too much and you needed time to heal."

"My point is that I've never seen Clayton as sullen and unhappy as he was in the days after he received your father's letter informing him that you had refused the marriage."

Thea frowned. "You must have mistaken it. Whatever reason Clayton was sullen had nothing to do with *my* absence, I assure you."

Phillip shifted in his chair and studied her. "Why do you say that?"

"Perhaps you do not know he was engaged to be married to another woman." Her faced heated as she said the words.

"Are you talking about Lady Lydia Malcolm?" Phillip asked.

"Lydia Malcolm? Is that who it was?" A mental image of Lady Lydia flashed through Thea's mind. She'd met the young woman before. Blond, graceful, beautiful. Perfect manners. Why, *she'd* want to marry Lady Lydia if *she* were a bachelor. No wonder Ewan was unhappy to have had to take Thea instead.

"Yes, and the truth is that they were never even engaged. Not formally."

"What?" A rush of heat like lightning flashed through Thea's middle.

Phillip splayed his hands across the table. "If he'd been engaged, you'd have seen it in the papers, wouldn't you?"

Thea shook her head. "I thought perhaps we missed it. Maggie doesn't always read me every line."

"It's true that Clayton and Lydia's father had discussed a possible match, but nothing was ever put to paper. And furthermore, I can assure you that Clayton never even mentioned Lydia to me more than once."

Thea took a deep breath. She closed her eyes. "You don't understand, Phillip. My mother always told me not to marry a man who didn't love me. Ewan cannot possibly love me."

Phillip studied her face. "I cannot tell you whether Ewan loves you. The answer to that is in his heart. But I can tell you that he was far from madly in love with Lydia Malcolm."

Thea swallowed hard. "May I ask you something else? There's something I must know."

"Of course." Phillip nodded.

"Does…does Ewan have a mistress in London?"

Phillip's crack of laughter was her first answer. "Clayton? A mistress? No. No. He's never been the sort."

Relief unlike anything Thea had ever known before poured through her veins. She expelled her breath. "Are you certain?"

"As certain as I can be," Phillip assured her.

For the first time since after the Christmastide ball, hope rose in Thea's chest. As Phillip said, it didn't mean that Ewan loved her, but at least he wasn't in love with *another* woman. But Thea still had to be certain. "Phillip, you said yourself, you can't know what's in his heart. Is it possible that he loved Lydia and just never mentioned her to you?"

Phillip leaned across the table and met her gaze. "I know this. I never heard him utter a word about Lydia, but after you left that morning, Thea, Ewan never stopped talking about *you*."

# CHAPTER FORTY-THREE

Ewan rode back to the stables that afternoon atop Midnight. Phillip was beside him riding Alabaster. Phillip had finally gone from speaking to the horse to riding him again. The duke had insisted, and Ewan was nothing but pleased with his friend's progress. He was getting closer and closer to being ready to re-enter Society and take his rightful place.

"I spoke to Thea earlier," Phillip said casually.

"And?" Ewan asked. He did his best to appear nonchalant, but he'd been waiting for Phillip to broach the topic ever since they'd left on their ride an hour earlier.

"And you're both fools if you ask me." Phillip leaned down and patted Alabaster's neck.

"Fools? Both of us?" Ewan retorted, chuckling.

"Yes," was Phillip's steadfast reply.

Ewan sauntered closer. "Very well, why is Thea a fool? I'd like to know."

Phillip lifted the reins. "Thea is a fool because she thinks you're in love with Lydia Malcolm."

"What?" Ewan scowled.

"Precisely." Phillip shook his head.

"How does Thea even *know* about Lydia Malcolm?" Ewan asked.

"I didn't ask her that. But she was convinced that not only were you engaged to Lydia, that you are also madly in love with the girl."

Ewan wrinkled his nose. "Where in God's name did Thea get that idea?"

"Where do fools get any of their ideas?" Phillip replied, a half-smile on his lips.

Ewan sighed and shook his head. "Very well, go ahead. Tell me why I'm a fool."

"With pleasure," Phillip continued, spurring the Arabian into the stables. "*You* are a fool because you haven't told your wife how you feel about her."

"What?" The scowl returned to Ewan's face.

"I don't know whether you love her. Though I suspect you do. But what does a bachelor like me know about love? I do, however, know that you couldn't stop talking about her and moping about this house after Thea left, and I told her as much."

"What? Why?" Ewan trotted up to the stablehand who was patiently waiting for them.

"Because she needed to hear it. Only she really needs to hear it from *you*," Phillip continued.

Ewan cursed under his breath. "Damn it, Harlowe. What are you saying?"

Phillip swung himself from the horse's back and landed on the packed earth. "I'm saying you should bloody well tell your wife that you love her, you idiot!"

～

LATER THAT DAY, after Ewan saw to the horses, he strode into the house and up to his bedchamber. After Phillip and Alabaster had returned to the stables, Ewan had ridden Midnight again for miles and miles trying to put to rights the rioting thoughts in his head. He'd got no more clarity than he'd had when he'd left, but at least he'd worn himself out.

He would bathe, dress, and hopefully have dinner with his wife. She couldn't hide from him forever. What sort of marriage would they have? One in which they barely spoke during the day and made passionate love at night? That's not what he wanted. Well, that wasn't *all* that he wanted. He wanted the young woman who'd laughed with him, joked with him, spoken to him about scientific theories and her mother. He wanted Thea, all of her.

He took a steaming bath. When he emerged from the tub, he wrapped a towel around his hips. As soon as the footmen finished emptying the tub and removing it from his bedchamber, he dismissed them. A soft knock sounded on the door from Thea's bedchamber.

"Come in," he called.

Thea opened the door. Her eyes widened as soon as she saw his state of undress. But instead of leaving, he could have sworn he saw a twinkle in her eye. She continued walking directly toward him.

"Would you like me to come back later?" she asked.

He glanced down at his towel and then back up at her. "No. Why?" He gave her a devilish grin.

She shrugged and continued to walk toward where he stood at the foot of the bed. "Very well. I came here to talk to you."

"About what?"

"About the fact that I've been an idiot," Thea replied.

Ewan grinned at her. "That is extremely convenient."

"Why's that?" she asked, cocking her head to the side.

"Because I was planning to talk to you about the same thing. Er, well, the fact that *I've* been an idiot, I mean."

"Oh, good, you go first." Thea clasped her hands together in front of her and blinked at him expectantly.

Ewan chuckled. "No. No. Ladies first, of course." Despite his state of undress, he bowed to her.

Thea nodded. "Very well. I spoke with Phillip today and he told me that you aren't in love with Lady Lydia Malcolm."

Ewan frowned. "Yes, he mentioned it. But I must ask, why would you think I was in love with Lydia? How did you even know about Lydia?"

Thea blushed. "I was... Well, you see... I was listening outside your study door the morning Father came after the story about us appeared in the paper. I heard you say you'd need to cry off from your *fiancée*."

Ewan expelled his breath. "I was never actually betrothed to Lydia."

"Yes, but you had an understanding with her father, did you not?"

"That's true. But love was certainly never part it."

Thea turned away from him. "I didn't know that. I thought perhaps you had affection for her at the least and were in love with her at the most."

Ewan sighed. "Did you ever think to ask me?"

Thea whirled to face him again. "That is precisely why I'm an idiot. I've been racked with guilt, all these weeks. Ever since I showed up in your stables and broke my leg. It's all been my fault. All of it. If I hadn't been sneaking around, you never would have been forced to marry me."

Ewan crossed his bare feet together at the ankles. "You're forgetting that you initially refused to marry me, and we weren't forced into it until I arrived at your home and kissed you in the sitting room."

"I only knew I thought you wanted Lydia. Until Phillip told me the truth." Thea's voice was tentative.

Ewan winced. "What exactly did Phillip tell you?"

"He told me that you missed me, you talked about me, you wished I hadn't gone." She blushed. "He said you never spoke of Lydia."

Ewan put a hand on his hip. "That is true. Lydia's father is well-connected. I thought of the match as a political decision. I suppose I was angry when the story first appeared in the papers because my ambition was about to be thwarted and that had never happened to me before. That's why I mentioned it to your father that day. But Thea, you must believe me when I tell you that I've long since discovered that ambition is nothing compared to...love."

Thea sucked in her breath. "Love?"

Ewan nodded and a lock of wet hair fell over one eye. He brushed it aside. "Before I met you, I never even guessed that I could marry for love, I—"

"What did you just say?" She swallowed.

"Damn it, Thea. I might as well admit it. I think I've been in love with you since the day you arrived on my doorstep and tried to convince me to sell you my horse."

She shook her head vehemently. "No. That cannot be. I was a selfish monster the entire time."

"Yes, you were. But how much better have I behaved? I may have taken you in and helped you with your leg, but it's not as if I was ignorant about the potential for scandal. I knew as well as you did that it could end the way it did."

"But...you disliked me. I know you did," she countered.

"Perhaps, at first." He chuckled. "But I'd never met anyone like you before. You knew what you wanted, and you were so confident and certain of yourself. When you started sneaking into my stables, I couldn't believe your audacity. When Bell came to visit, he told me it sounded as if I was in love. I couldn't disagree. That's why I came to your Christmastide ball."

Thea's hand flew to her throat. "That's why?"

"I missed you. I had to see you. I wanted to hear from you exactly why you refused me." Ewan turned and paced away from her. "You asked me once what I thought of you that first day. You were stubborn, yes, but I also thought you were magnificent. Magnificent and gorgeous, so like the horse you were so desperate to win." Ewan turned back toward her and stepping forward, he pulled her into his arms and stared down into her eyes. "I've always thought you were magnificent, Thea. And I always will." He kissed her deeply.

After Ewan's lips finally left hers, Thea said softly. "My father isn't particularly well connected in Parliament."

Ewan nuzzled at her ear. "It doesn't matter. I love you madly."

Thea closed her eyes and leaned her head back. "I love you too, Ewan."

He pulled away from her to watch her face. "You don't have to say that if you don't mean it."

She shook her head. "I wouldn't do that. I think I fell in love with you when you were so nice to me after I broke my leg. You could have called the constable, you could have sent me away, instead you treated me as a true guest, a friend even. You brought me the wheelchair and asked me about myself. When I went back home, I realized the truth of how I felt about you. I was just too blindly stubborn to admit that being stubborn can cost you something you dearly love if you're not careful. I was so certain Father didn't want the best for me. I never even stopped to consider what *I* thought was the best for me. But the last thing I wanted to do was to force you into a marriage you didn't want. I would run away first."

"Yes, your father mentioned that to me in his letter. But

don't think too poorly of your father, my darling. The morning we were married he admitted to me that he'd insisted you stay at my house with your broken leg because he hoped we'd make a match."

"What?" Thea's mouth fell open. "Of all the despicable— He thought the only way to make a man want me would be to stick me under his roof for weeks?"

"Something like that," Ewan allowed with a grin. "But it worked, didn't it?"

Laughing, Thea leaned up on tiptoes, wrapped her arms around Ewan's neck and kissed him again. "Hmm. You're right. Perhaps Father isn't all bad after all. I'll have to thank him next time I see him, I suppose."

Ewan squeezed her against his nearly naked body. "Let's not make plans quite so soon. He told me he hoped a grandchild would be on the way the next time he saw either of us. I'd like to accommodate him."

Thea gasped. "He didn't say that!"

"He most certainly did."

Thea shook her head. "Why, that scheming man. I had no idea he'd planned the whole thing."

"Well, he didn't plan the bit about me winning the horse auction. I suppose I'll just have to always wonder whether you only married me for one reason and one reason only." He rubbed his nose against hers. "My horse."

Thea burst out laughing. "You rogue. I did no such thing. I would have scrimped and saved for years to purchase that horse. But once I saw how happy Alabaster made Phillip, I knew I had to leave them together."

"On the contrary," Ewan said, kissing Thea on the neck, "Phillip gave him to us as a wedding gift."

Thea tilted her head to the side to allow him better access. "He didn't need to do that."

"I told him the same thing, but he insisted," Ewan continued, trailing his lips down to her *décolletage*.

Thea's breath was coming in short pants. Her eyes closed. "Well, he can certainly visit and ride him as much as he chooses."

"I agree, my love." Ewan's was already unbuttoning the back of her gown. "Now, if you'd like, let me show you how to ride *me*."

Thea's eyes widened. "Ooh, I love the sound of that."

# CHAPTER FORTY-FOUR

The next afternoon, Ewan, Thea, and Phillip were having tea in one of the sitting rooms. The newly married couple had just finished thanking Phillip for his generous wedding gift of Alabaster. They'd also just finished informing Phillip that thanks to him calling them both fools, they'd talked and were quite happy together and madly in love with each other.

"I owe you both far more than a horse and some well-timed advice," Phillip replied.

"You owe us nothing," Ewan declared.

"I quite agree." Thea nodded and wrapped one arm around her husband's broad shoulders.

Before Phillip could reply, the door to the sitting room opened and Beau Bellham strode inside.

Ewan glanced up. "Good afternoon, Bell. We were wondering where you'd got off to." Ewan rose from his seat and shook the marquess's hand.

"I've been quite busy today," Bell replied, bowing to Thea and paying his respects, before exchanging pleasantries with Phillip as well.

"Oh, really," Ewan replied. He'd made his way to the sideboard where he poured a glass of water for his friend. "Doing what?"

Bell took the glass that Ewan offered him. "I've solved one of our two mysteries."

"Two mysteries?" Thea repeated, blinking.

"Yes," Bell replied. "The first was the identity of the culprit who provided the story of you staying here to the *Times*, Lady Thea."

Thea leaned forward in her seat. "You know the answer to that? Do tell. The truth is I've believed all this time that it was Rosalie, the house maid."

"It wasn't Rosalie," Bell replied with a grin. "My sources told me it was Lord Theodore Harding."

"Uncle Teddy!" Thea nearly shouted. "Are you certain?"

"Certain as I can be," Bell replied, taking a sip from his glass.

Thea tapped her cheek with one finger. "Why, Uncle Teddy didn't even know I was here until…right before the story came out in the paper," she finished, her irritation with her uncle growing by the moment. "Why in the world would my own uncle do that to me?"

"I took the liberty of visiting him at your father's house this morning and asking him that very question, my lady," Bell replied.

Ewan looked at Thea and shrugged. "What can I say? Bell is a thorough spy."

Thea gave Bell a wary glance. "What did Uncle Teddy say?"

"He told me that you'd taken far too long to find a husband and that your father had written him telling him that your stay here was the best chance you had to make a decent match at last and if you should write him and ask him to come fetch you, Teddy should refuse."

"My father told him that? What in the world!" Thea shook her head. "I suppose I shouldn't be surprised, but I am."

"I told you he wanted us together, darling," Ewan said, placing his hand on Thea's shoulder.

Thea covered Ewan's hand with hers. "Yes, I knew it, but I'd no idea he'd written to Uncle Teddy. The man has no shame."

"I'd say your uncle is the one without shame," Bell continued. "Apparently, it was entirely his idea to involve the papers. He thought that would settle the issue for certain."

Thea's mouth formed a wide O. "I cannot believe—"

"Don't be too angry with them, Thea," Phillip said to her with a laugh. "In the end it's worked out splendidly and that's what matters."

Thea sighed. "I suppose you're right. But don't think my uncle won't hear an earful the next time I see him."

"I would expect nothing less from you, darling," Ewan said, leaning over and kissing her soundly on the cheek.

Thea hugged Ewan before turning back to face Bell. "You mentioned two mysteries, Lord Bellingham. What's the second one?"

"I'm afraid the second one may have to do with me," Phillip interjected, shifting uncomfortably in his chair.

"Oh? What don't I know?" Thea asked, turning to face her friend.

"That's why Bell is here," Ewan continued. "In addition to attending the wedding, I asked him to come so we could make our final plans for Phillip's return to Society."

Thea searched Phillip's face. "You're feeling strong enough to return to Society? To take your rightful place?"

"Yes." Phillip nodded. "I am finally feeling strong enough. Thanks to you and Clayton…and Alabaster, my lady."

Thea squeezed her friend's hand. "You did the most difficult part, Phillip."

"Yes, well, I'm afraid there will be more difficulty ahead," Bell said ominously.

"I'm certain it will be difficult for you, Phillip," Thea continued. "What with your brother dying so suddenly. Being the duke is not something you'd ever planned, I'm certain."

"Yes well, that's just it," Phillip replied, exchanging a fraught glance with the other two men.

Thea furrowed her brow. Her gaze jumped between all three of the others. "What? What are you not telling me?"

Phillip took a deep breath and clapped his hands over his knees. "Bell and Clayton here don't believe my brother died suddenly."

"It's true," Bell replied. "The former Duke of Harlowe was murdered. And I intend to see his murderer brought to justice."

Thea's wide-eyed gaze swung to Ewan's. Her husband nodded. "It's true. And not only that, but we believe the man who killed the duke may try to kill Phillip as well."

Thank you for reading *Save a Horse, Ride a Viscount*. Please page forward to see related books, my biography, and how to contact me!

*Valerie*

ALSO BY VALERIE BOWMAN

Thank you for reading
*Save a Horse, Ride a Viscount.*
I hope you enjoyed Ewan and Thea's story.
When I began writing this book, all I knew was that she broke her leg doing something with his horse and the rest just magically emerged from my fingertips as I typed. Ha!

I'd love to keep in touch.

- Visit my website for information about upcoming books, excerpts, and to sign up for my email newsletter: www.ValerieBowmanBooks.com or at www.ValerieBowmanBooks.com/subscribe.
- Join me on Facebook: http://Facebook.com/ValerieBowmanAuthor.
- Reviews help other readers find books. I appreciate all reviews whether positive or negative. Thank you so much for considering it!

Want to read the other Footmen's Club books?

- The Footman and I
- Duke Looks Like a Groomsman
- The Valet Who Loved Me

# ABOUT THE AUTHOR

Valerie Bowman grew up in Illinois with six sisters (she's number seven) and a huge supply of historical romance novels.

After a cold and snowy stint earning a degree in English with a minor in history at Smith College, she moved to Florida the first chance she got.

Valerie now lives in Jacksonville with her family including her two rascally dogs. When she's not writing, she keeps busy reading, traveling, or vacillating between watching crazy reality TV and PBS.

Valerie loves to hear from readers. Find her on the web at www.ValerieBowmanBooks.com.

facebook.com/ValerieBowmanAuthor
twitter.com/ValerieGBowman
instagram.com/valeriegbowman
goodreads.com/Valerie_Bowman
pinterest.com/ValerieGBowman
bookbub.com/authors/valerie-bowman
amazon.com/author/valeriebowman

CPSIA information can be obtained
at www.ICGtesting.com
Printed in the USA
LVHW031925130521
687356LV00007B/854

9 781736 841716